LAEVIUM

THE CERULEAN AIRSHIP - BOOK ONE

RUXANDRA TARCA

Laevium © 2020 Ruxandra Tarca

All Rights Reserved.
No part of this book may be reproduced in any form or by any electronic or mechanical means, including information storage and retrieval systems, without permission in writing from the author. The only exception is by a reviewer, who may quote short excerpts in a review.

This book is a work of fiction. All names, characters, places, and incidents either are products of the author's imagination or are used fictitiously. Any resemblance to actual persons, living or dead, events, or locales is entirely coincidental.

Ruxandra Tarca
www.delifictional.com

Cover art by Alina Popovici
www.alinapopovici.com

First Edition: Bucharest, December 2020
ISBN 978-973-0-33278-0 (paperback)
ISBN 978-973-0-33279-7 (ebook)

1

London, June 1895

Jasper Kendall Asher decided it was about time he got out of his plain wooden bed. That day he had to work in the clocktower, so being late was unthinkable.

He stretched his arms and pushed the windows of the small chamber wide open, letting in the morning air tinged with the salty odour of the Thames.

The lively noises coming from the docks invigorated him. Fully awake, he went to the washbasin and poured the cold content of the ewer over his head and bare shoulders, relishing the chilly water on his skin.

Without bothering too much to tame his unkempt black hair, he donned his brown corduroy trousers and white collarless shirt and left the room.

Downstairs, the mess in his workshop made quite a deplorable picture. Clocks, dials, cables, cogs of all sizes, and devices of more or less strange shapes were scattered everywhere in a mixture of brass, wood, and copper. On his workbench, Mrs Carraway had left a breakfast tray like she did every day, disregarding his relentless attempts to convince her that he never ate in the morning. He only picked an apple and stepped outside.

Soon, the river opened before him.

He glanced at the crowded tiered platforms of the Blackfriars Bridge Skystation.

It's still early. If I walk, I should be at the clocktower in Westminster in half an hour.

With the hustle and bustle of the wharves slowly receding behind, Jasper looked up at the suspended tracks bending towards Holborn. He still remembered that spring day, five years earlier, when the first gondotram used those rails under the curious eyes of the people who had gathered to welcome the bizarre iron monster which would quickly spread across the entire capital.

A shrilling noise signalled the wagon-like vehicle passing high above. Hauled by giant cogwheels thrust forward by the power of steam, it resembled a reverted train on an upside down railway.

The city had changed a lot during the last ten years since the Reform transformed the society entirely, and the Orders had become the second ruling entity in England, heralding a time of significant changes.

With its trains and tube, its carriages pulled by mechanical horses, and its aerial gondotrams, London had become a hub of technological wonders at the dawn of the new century. Omnibuses were almost history. Only a few remained, in Whitechapel and some other destitute corners Londoners of good breeding preferred to avoid.

Jasper arrived at the clocktower that dominated Parliament Square, close to the Inspectorates building. The cogwheels needed checking and oiling twice a year, and when the time came, his master saw nothing else around.

The old clock had to be more accurate than the finest pocket watch.

"Good morning, Master Hollingsworth," Jasper greeted the man who was dismantling parts of the humongous mechanism up in the clock room.

"Welcome, dear boy." The royal mechanic looked at his former apprentice, adjusting his pince-nez. "Would you be so kind as to lend me a hand with this old lady?"

"Is this really the last time we oil it this year?" Jasper asked, helping him pull a fat cog out of its axis. "If I am to believe Edmund's message, the inspection in September is cancelled."

"The Earl of Wyverstone informed you right. He requested some new implement for this clock, and I need to test it here undisturbed. Hence, no more checks this year."

"Whatever for? My brother never asks for anything without reason."

"He wants me to devise an alarm and place it among the cogwheels to trigger the tower bells if someone covertly attempts to get close to any of the clockfaces."

"Why would he want to keep people away? This tower offers the best view of the city."

Theophilus Hollingsworth beckoned Jasper to follow him into the narrow space that circled the entire perimeter of the tower, between the walls and the clockfaces. He stopped before one of the small windows which made the transparent dials.

"This place can also be the best spot to throw a gunpowder bomb or to shoot," the old man said. "Something. Or someone. The envelope of a balloon. Or the passengers of an airship."

"I wonder what my brother is hiding this time." Jasper frowned. "Always his bloody secrets! If Edmund believes someone could come here to throw bombs at passengers on airships, his fears must be real."

"Especially when the passengers have the highest rank in England, dear boy. Her Majesty wants a new airship, which she intends to inaugurate next spring at the Engineers World Gathering. Imagine how many influential people will witness that ship's maiden flight over London – members of the Royal House included. Your brother needs to make sure nothing inauspicious happens again."

So that was it! Jasper clenched his fists. *The Royal House wants a new airship to brag about at the most important technological event in the world, and Edmund is in charge? As if the Griffin never existed?*

The memory of a burning night sky, of an airship disintegrating before even touching the ground, gripped his chest, vivid as if it occurred only the day before. In three years, no one had bothered to investigate. That was something impossible to forget or forgive.

Jasper felt the pangs of a terrible headache. He had stayed away from his brother's affairs for a long while. Now he expected to be dragged into one of them again, without having much of a say. He knew his brother better than anyone. If Edmund Asher, Earl of Wyverstone, believed there was the slightest chance for something bad to happen, then it could happen. And, in the particular case no one took action, most of the times it *did* happen.

"Have they forgotten about *The Golden Griffin*?" Jasper asked, his voice unsteady. "Jade and all the others who died on Her Majesty's airship mean nothing to the Royal House? Or to Edmund? Are they only rotten bones to them? Don't they at least deserve we learn the truth so that they can rest in peace?

"For Heaven's sake, that ship was rigged, and the

Inspectorates just closed the case! Without a proper investigation!"

"You do not know what is going on behind the closed doors of your brother's office," Theophilus Hollingsworth said. "Try to trust him more. He will tell you everything when the time comes, for you will play a part in this. You should return into service."

"I am not sure I *want* to play a part in this. Shouldn't this airship be the duty of the Engineers Order? Why is Edmund involved?"

"To counter the Marquess of Leythfordham's influence. The Engineers Order and some of the most powerful noble families in England are backing him. He covets the official assignment for Her Majesty's new airship, and the Queen's trust in your brother is the only thing that stopped him from getting it. But I don't know for how long the earl will be able to hold him back."

"I've heard the marquess wants to build a new airharbour in the city," Jasper said. "He is attempting to buy everyone's support to tear down the former rookery in St. Giles. Progress, he says, but he only wants a little exclusive playground for the aristocracy. At the expense of all those unfortunate souls who live there."

"I hope he won't receive any encouragement for that nonsense," the royal mechanic said. "His father is the Duke of Litchborough, he is ambitious and infamously wealthy but has no power without the peers' approval. However, he is gathering support within the Engineers Order. Quite a few members are willing to help him become Her Majesty's official airship engineer. Even the Senior Lord of the Order would allow that."

"Benedict Quimby favours such a ridiculous idea?" A glint of amusement sparkled in Jasper's blue eyes. "Has the almighty Senior Lord of the Engineers Order gone mad? How could Leythfordham be the official engineer of the Royal House? He cannot even tell one craft from another!"

"I agree. But the support he receives from the Engineers Order is real. To question Quimby's authority is difficult, and Edmund doesn't have much time. We want Her Majesty's airship to be not only safe but also the best – which is impossible if the chief engineer is Alexis McQuillian, Marquess of Leythfordham. I see only one way to have the most astounding engineering project at the Gathering."

"Which is?"

"Which is for you to return as a fully active member of the Order and in Her Majesty's service. We need your help."

"Her Majesty's new airship is not my concern."

"Nor is our country's reputation?"

"I am too insignificant to have a say in our country's reputation. Tell me about this trap my brother requested. What are you planning?"

The old mechanic didn't push the issue further. "I shall connect it to the entrance to the clockfaces, and the bells above. If anyone tries to enter this space without pulling a hidden lever to stop my mechanism, the door will lock behind them and the bells will chime. It will be a matter of minutes before someone from the Inspectorates comes to check what happened."

"I understand." Jasper started fiddling with a small cog, his eyes dark and unfocused. He knew what was coming, what his brother would expect of him, but he decided not to think about that yet.

The day passed with no notable events. When they finished, it was already evening. Jasper returned to the clockfaces corridor, leaning his forehead on the dial's glass to stare at the sunset.

A few pale sunbeams were piercing through the clouds that had covered the sky, reflecting into the river with a thin silvery glint. The people seemed small dolls walking around in a colourful blend of long dresses, trousers, bonnets, and hats. Steammotors, hansom cabs, and mechanical horses carriages were transporting their passengers to all the corners of the city.

Nearby, the red brick building of the Inspectorates was looming like an enormous shadow over the entire square. Edmund must be there in his office on the second floor, engrossed in some secret work known only to a few people.

Jasper's eyes rested on the airharbour. In the distance, he distinguished the airships' outlines against the sunset. Cargo, cruisers, long-distance, landing or taking off from their berths. All kinds of ships, bigger or smaller, each with her own shape, and crew, and story.

"You miss it, isn't that so? Being an airship engineer." His master's voice almost startled him. "Never thought of returning to the skies? Or to your workbench? Idle repair work doesn't suit you, dear boy. You are only twenty-two years of age. You still have so much to show to the world!"

"I have nothing to show to a world that forbids me to find out why my twin brother died," Jasper said bitterly, eager to end that conversation. He kept looking far into the distance until the yellow gleam of the streetlamps completely took over the daylight.

JASPER'S POCKET watch showed nine o'clock when he opened the door at the Copper Kettle. Any sane person avoided Seven Dials after dark. Yet, he felt comfortable among those impoverished people who had helped him more than once when he sought refuge from his anger after Jade's death on *The Golden Griffin*.

He was a regular of that place, where nobody questioned the smears on his face or the oil and soot on his clothes after a day's work among cogwheels, levers, and iron bars. They had accepted him, although he wasn't one of them by birth. The streetwalkers, crooks, beggars, and ragamuffins in that part of St. Giles were his other family, one he came to understand and love.

Inside, the thick smoke almost materialised into a grey blanket floating up to the beamed ceiling, covering the odour of sweat, alcohol, and cheap food that saturated the walls. The buzz of conversation mixed up with the clank of glasses and pints, making it hard to distinguish one word from another in the general murmur.

"Master Jasper!" a meaty bald man behind the bar shouted the moment he saw him coming in. "Had a hard day, ain't it so? What to be? Double gin or beer?"

"A double!" Jasper replied, making his way to the counter. "Add some cheese and potatoes. I'm starving!"

"Today they called good ol' Jack at the docks!" one customer shouted, pointing to a lanky man standing next to him. "He'll put some bread on that table of his. If he doesn't spend all his coins on gin and beer, that is!"

"Blimey, Hector!" Jack grunted, half pleased and half embarrassed. "I'll go again tomorrow. I 'eard vey need workers for some new factory. If I'm lucky, maybe vey take me. Good pay."

"The families get good dough, vey do. But none of the men who went there returned yet, and no one can tell where the factory is. Ain't a good place, that one. Better stay wiv yer children, Jack."

Jasper smiled, taking a sip of gin. He knew how hard Jack

Killen struggled, how he hunted daily jobs at the docks or the airharbour, how the quay gangers ignored him in favour of sturdier men. He barely earned enough for his two boys to live from hand to mouth. A day of work gave him enough reasons to celebrate.

"Jack, go home, and I'll pay for your drink. The children must be waiting for you."

"Aye, Master Jasper. Little 'uns are happy. Vey're going to Lady Hollingsworth's school. Me vife told me she came vis afternoon, wiv clothes and food. An angel, God bless 'er."

Another family would benefit from Rowena Hollingsworth's charity. Since the Reform established the new aerial gondotram system and the airharbour, many shanty areas in London had become rather tolerable. Yet, in places like Whitechapel and St. Giles, people still needed help. Jack was right. His master's daughter was the closest he knew to an angel.

"You lot, have you ever thought of moving out of St. Giles?" Jasper asked, attracting several baffled eyes upon him.

"Why would we?" Jack looked like he had just heard the joke of the day. "St. Giles ain't for the faint of heart, but it's still our home. 'ow can we leave?"

"It's dirty, and not all the people is good 'uns, but we're happy here," Hector added. "Look around, and you won't see nuffing else but whores, pickpockets and ruffians. All kinds of blokes and miscreants. But we wouldn't trade this place for any other, as poor and filthy as it is."

St. Giles wasn't the best place to be, but it was those people's home. There was no way in hell that bastard of Leythfordham would have it torn down. He would not allow it, even though it meant working with Edmund again.

A hand landed on his nape, and he turned around to see a young woman wearing a low-cut red dress underneath a black leather corset. A layer of heavy makeup was partially hiding her features, and her black hair was spilling over her bare shoulders and arms.

"You look like a chimney sweep," she said, sliding her fingers under his shirt. "You could use some hot water and a warm bed. Tonight, I happen to have both."

"Insolent harlot! How dare you talk to Master Jasper like that!" the bald bartender bellowed. "Know your place!"

"Why are you here, Hazel?" Jasper eyed her doubtfully – she didn't come there too often. "Is anything the matter?"

"Nothing in particular. Madame sent me to bring her a thing or two, and I dropped by for a glass of gin."

She was on a mission, one of those routine information gathering outings Hazel usually did for her Madame. In another time, they used to help him as well.

"Send Carmina my regards. Perhaps I should call on her one of these days."

"That I will. You last crossed our doorstep so long ago that it's a wonder if Madame still remembers your lovely face."

Jasper thought about the owner of the Cinnamon Dove, the establishment close to Covent Garden.

I bet she does. Such a witty woman never forgets anyone or anything. Carmina Harcourt is one of the best information sources in underground London. And the best partner I ever had.

~

JASPER RETURNED to his house on Tallis Street tired and half drunk, determined to sleep through the entire following day. He wouldn't open the workshop. It needed some serious cleaning anyway.

He pressed a small knob, and the murky yellow light of the elliptical bulb flooded the room.

His eyes fell on a folded sheet of paper that hadn't been on the desk in the morning. Frowning, he took the note, read it, and threw it into the wastebasket.

In less than ten minutes, he was in his room, still dressed in the dirty clothes he had worn over the day, fast asleep.

2

"Rats and caterpillars! Not now!" The leather strap fell over her chest, hanging from the metallic buckle. "Eudora, bring the damned sewing basket! The blasted thing came off again!"

Prompted by the angry yell, a plump short woman in her late fifties entered the small drawing room carrying a wicker basket.

"God have mercy on us, Miss Ivy!" She put her load on the only table in the room. "What language is that, mind you? Your poor parents would bleed to hear their daughter talking like a Whitechapel bloke! This is not how a lady behaves!"

"I ain't no lady," Ivy said, squinting at her nursemaid.

"You are an educated young woman," Eudora Carraway scolded, sewing the corset strap back into place. "You studied in Paris, and your parents were among the finest scientists in the Engineers Order of Her Majesty."

"Tell me, how did you get us that breakfast today?" Ivy's green eyes were glittering with annoyance.

"Master Jasper left his food untouched again in the

workshop. I found it when I cleaned his house last night. Thought it was a pity to let it spoil."

"That's what I'm saying! It's not my parents who will feed us! They are dead! We barely scrape a living, our house is three streets away from one of the worst slums left in London, I can't afford new flying gear, and we're happy to eat other people's leftovers. Is this the time to be thinking of my upbringing? Or my education?"

"We still have a roof over our heads, and your airship. We should be thankful for that. Here, I finished. Your strap."

Ivy Blackwell went to the tall mirror, a stark reminder of her dire circumstances. The dark brown leather corset covered her creamy short-sleeved chemise, its straps now well fixed over her shoulders. A canvas overskirt hid the layers of puffy beige petticoats of her knee-long aeronaut costume, mended way too many times. The boots completed the desolate view, their original colour long forgotten.

She tied her auburn wavy hair and fastened her goggles on top of her head.

"I'm off!" Ivy threw a compass, an aeronaut cap, and a notebook in her bag. "Tonight, I shall return with a few good shillings even if it means begging them to choose my ship!"

Out in the street, Ivy stared at the small house she had from her late parents. Eudora was right. They were lucky to have a roof over their heads, shabby and sparingly furnished as it was. The exterior painting had fallen in many places, making the walls look like they had some kind of terminal illness. She didn't have the means to take care of it, but it didn't matter. It was the only place she could call home.

That morning, the young aeronaut felt particularly bitter. She had spent almost all the money left from her parents, and she hated to depend on her nursemaid. At almost nineteen, she was still unmarried and without a stable income. The Reform and its changes had saved her. In the old days, she would have been just a wallflower too old to grab a husband, confined by the rigid laws of the society and unable to earn her own money.

She could sell the plans of her parents' new – though unfinished – airship, but they were Octavia and Chalford Blackwell's most valuable work, the research of their last year of life. Everyone believed those documents had disappeared along with her parents that blasted night on *The Golden Griffin* – the last of their completed projects.

Yet, she dreaded that, one day, the Engineers or Aviators Orders would learn the truth and claim them. She had to keep them safe until she saved enough to turn those plans into a real airship. But first she had to make ends meet. The flying season had just started, which meant many people ready to pay well just to hover over London for a couple of hours.

Ivy walked up the massive metal stairs to the third deck of the Blackfriars Bridge Skystation, grudgingly fishing for two coins in a pocket. She inserted them into the brass slot of an accessway to the suspended tracks and pulled the lever. The small wrought iron fence rolled to the right, allowing her to step onto Platform 7. High above, the copper sign read *Blackfriars Bridge – Airharbour-bound.*

In less than a minute, the gondotram coming from Waterloo stopped at the platform. The doors slid, letting a flood of people in and out. From her spot at the window, Ivy gazed at the landscape below, oblivious to the crowd around.

~

IVY HURRIED to the red brick building next to the airharbour entrance. Two other aviators were coming out, papers in hand, looking at her as if she were some kind of oddity. How pitiful she must seem in their eyes, wearing that old gear and always begging for assignments, no matter how small.

She entered the stuffy office of the airharbour clerk, putting on her best smile.

"Good morning, Hayes. Do you have anything for me?"

The old man frowned, looking over his thick spectacles.

"Miss Blackwell, I'm afraid I have just assigned the last two jobs available for today. But worry not. The season has just started, and the offer will be plentiful."

Ivy stared at him as if she hadn't understood the meaning of his words. He couldn't possibly tell her she had come there for nothing. It would be the fourth damned day in a row. Soon, she wouldn't be able to afford even the gondotram, and she didn't fancy walking all the way there. She needed money, which she couldn't get if the Assignments Office kept ignoring her airship.

She did her best to keep her temper. "You are avoiding giving me work, are you not? Perhaps I should remind you I paid the yearly subscription, so I have as much right to receive jobs as any other aviator whose craft is berthed here."

"I give priority to the members of the Aviators Order. If you want to secure a place on the roster, get yourself registered."

Like she could. She had no registration money, and *The Skycradle* still belonged to her parents in the papers. As if erasing her existence in Paris, making her live there under another identity, wasn't enough. The mess left by her mother and father maddened her.

"You know I can't!" she snapped, giving up any pretence of civility. "I am not asking for the best passenger group that filed a request. I just want a *bloody assignment*! Even a cargo would do!"

"Miss Blackwell, please mind your manners. It is most disheartening to hear a respectable young woman yelling like that."

"I don't give a rusted screw on how disheartened you are!" She would at least have that bit of satisfaction to spit it all in his face. "I'm paying my fees, so I'm expecting equal treatment, Aviators Order or not!"

"Look here, Miss Blackwell. We offer the best services to our passengers. Have you checked your airship lately? When have you last painted her? Or inspected her envelope?"

The metallic chime of the speakerbox cut off Ivy's attempt to reply.

"Airharbour Assignments Office, this is Hadrian Hayes. How can I help you?" he answered in a mellow tone in the receiver, still glaring at Ivy.

"Oh, Your Ladyship will be most pleased to hear that we do. When can we expect you?"

Ivy glanced at the small box made of wood, brass and copper which she'd always wished to have. Yet, as common as speakerboxes had become in many houses throughout England, she still couldn't afford such an item.

"In one hour, then." Hayes returned the receiver onto the hook, his eyes on Ivy.

"You got an assignment. Her Ladyship Rowena Hollingsworth needs an airship for a few hours. She is the royal mechanic's daughter, and a highly regarded lady, so I suggest you keep your temper in place."

"Thank you, Hayes," Ivy said, smiling as if their previous argument didn't exist. "What must I do?"

"Nothing too difficult. Lady Hollingsworth wants to sponsor a flight over London for some unfortunate children in St. Giles. They have never been inside an airship before, and she'll pay well to change that."

At last, that night she would bring some shillings home.

~

The Skycradle had seen better days, but she was still impressive. If not in size – she was a small airship – most certainly in her design. The colour of her russet envelope had faded, yet was still bright enough to remind of her former glory.

Ivy was particularly proud of the gondola, fitted with parallel thin brass belts and attached to the envelope with rigid bars that made her seem a cradle in the sky. Close to the stabilisers in the back, a narrow ladder linked the crew hold to the small cargo space.

The oval door of the gondola slid aside, triggered by the five digits sequence of her cypher.

Throwing her bag in the pilot seat, Ivy went to the board for the pre-flight checks. The gauges came to life, indicating excellent gas and pressure levels. She pulled an iron lever, and the gondola's starboard wall came down halfway, revealing the observation deck. The girl propped her elbows on the railing and stared into the distance, filling her eyes with the beloved view of the airharbour.

"Miss Blackwell, I assume? I am Rowena Hollingsworth, I believe you were expecting us."

Ivy turned to the young woman standing in the gondola's doorway. A little taller than her, she wore a chestnut plaid dress, and from under her simple straw hat came out a mass of black curls. Ivy guessed she ought to be a few years older than her.

The guest took one step inside. "What a beautiful ship!"

Ivy tried to figure out whether her words carried any trace

of mockery. As she saw none, she offered her a tentative smile.

"She is, ain't it so?" Ivy said, right when two figures appeared from behind the elegant lady. Two boys, the youngest no more than ten years old and the oldest no more than twelve. Their clothes and boots were worn out and a tad too large, but they were clean. "Are these our little passengers?"

"Oh, please allow me to introduce the Killen siblings." Lady Hollingsworth pushed them gently in front of her. "Blake and Erik."

"Good day, Miss Blackwell," the children chanted in one voice, bowing hesitantly. Ivy's cheeks turned red under her freckles.

"This is their first day of school," Lady Hollingsworth said, while the children hurried to the observation deck. "Erik and Blake love airships. As little children, they used to chase those who passed above the narrow alleys of their neighbourhood. But they have never set foot in a craft."

"Aye, Yer Ladyship!" Erik yelled, his chin glued on the railing. "We wasn't nuffing higher than the gondotram. Miss aeronaut, will you take us to the skies?"

"Straight to the skies!" Ivy fixed her goggles, closed the gondola door, and returned to the navigation board. She pushed a big red knob, releasing the outer grapples that held *The Skycradle* in place in its berth. The engines started buzzing under her command.

In a few minutes, they were airborne.

London unfolded below them like a vast, colourful board where a masterful architect had placed buildings, trees, the docks, and the river winding its way throughout the city. The children squealed in delight each time they recognised a place.

"Look down there, Lady Rowena!" little Blake squeaked, while they were hovering over the Inspectorates. "Ain't that the Westminster clock? If we get closer, maybe we see Master Jasper in the tower!"

Without waiting for Lady Hollingsworth's answer and with no warning, Ivy swiftly manoeuvred *The Skycradle*. Soon, they were flying less than a metre distance from the clockfaces, grinning at the children's ecstatic shrieks.

"'Ow did you do that?" Erik asked in amazement. "Changing the course like that!"

"Sorcery!" Ivy laughed, while setting the airship on her return course to the airharbour. She liked her passengers. Their curious questions made her feel needed for the first time in a long while.

"Look!" Erik pointed his finger to a red spot in the distance. "What is happening there? I know that place!"

Lady Hollingsworth squinted in the direction he indicated. Her eyes filled with an unspoken fear.

"Miss Blackwell, could you please lower *The Skycradle*?"

Ivy didn't miss the urgency in her voice. She set the ship on a descending course, then looked at starboard through the magnifying lenses of her goggles.

"Rats and caterpillars!" she yelled in horror. "A building is falling!"

"I would be grateful if you could send the children home." Ivy sensed sheer panic behind Rowena's collected tone. "And if you could let me off here. A rope would do. Anything that can get me down there would do. That thing falling is the roof of my school."

3

Rowena Hollingsworth was running as if her life depended on it. Coming down *The Skycradle's* folding ladder had been a risky endeavour, but she had managed to land in one piece on the nearest rooftop.

With her hat lost, her face red and glistening, and her hair dishevelled in a most unladylike manner, she climbed down the narrow metal stairs affixed to the wall, gripping the iron wheels of the exterior exhaust ducts of the building for support.

As soon as she touched the ground, she grabbed her dirty skirts with one hand and rushed to the school as fast as her feet allowed.

Countless agonising thoughts were crossing her mind. How bad was it? Why did it fall? And the most dreadful question – what if one of the dear people who always helped her was inside?

When she arrived, all the air drained from her lungs. Half of what once had been the small building of her school had collapsed into a pile of red bricks, crumbled furniture and broken glass confined within a few roofless walls.

She looked around in dismay. “What in the Lord’s name happened here? Is anyone hurt?”

“God have mercy on us, Yer Ladyship!” a man said, coming out of the crowd who had gathered there. “We dunno yet, ‘twas closed when you left for the airharbour. But we ‘ear Jack Killen wanted to mend the tables while Yer Ladyship was away wiv his little ‘uns.”

Rowena hurried inside to search through the rubble along with the others. She dreaded to think the man might have died at her school.

“Lady Hollingsworth, please come out!” a woman yelled. “The wall could fall on you! We can’t know if Jack’s in there!”

“No, we cannot unless we search for him!” Rowena went further among broken bricks and cracked wood.

If anyone was inside, she would find them. It had taken her almost three years and a lot of pain and compromises to get her school of crafts running in a place everyone avoided. Her peers used to treat her with doubt and raised eyebrows. They either mocked or ignored her efforts to do something else for the poor instead of just throwing money at them.

In time, her patience had been rewarded. Her school’s former pupils were now working on ships, at the docks, or at the airharbour. Those people loved and trusted her.

Now, everything had turned to dust. Her brain couldn’t comprehend the enormity unfolding before her eyes.

“I don’t know what you lot are looking for, but if it’s me, I ain’t there,” Jack Killen said, who had just arrived along with a constable. “Nasty work, a good roof to fall like that.”

“If it was indeed as good as you say.” The constable turned to Rowena. “Lady Hollingsworth, I would like a word with you if you please. You endangered the lives of these people, forcing them to come to a school that was in a less than precarious state. What happened here today could have been a tragedy. I cannot let this pass."

Everyone gazed at him in astonishment. The constable's rudeness towards one of the most respectable ladies in London was outrageous. Unlike many of noble birth, Rowena never flaunted her title, preferring to make her presence almost unnoticed. But the way that man in uniform addressed her was irritating.

She straightened her back.

"Sir, I do not recall us being introduced. Given the emergency of the situation, I shall overlook this impertinence I would not have otherwise dismissed with such ease. *However*, I cannot ignore your words. I believe you did *not* mean to say I *forced* these people to receive *proper education* at my school, in a building that was in *excellent* condition. Since I am *terribly distressed*, I must have misunderstood."

The sheer power of her steely voice and the icy look in her eyes made the constable falter. The others watched in awe the Lady Hollingsworth they adored. Kind and sweet, but as unyielding as iron when needed.

The policeman bowed. "Your Ladyship, please forgive my rudeness. I rushed into conclusions which were obviously out of place."

"Indeed. Now I would like to find out what happened here. I hope I can count on your willingness and abilities for that."

~

ALMOST THREE O'CLOCK in the afternoon and the gondotram wagon was as crowded as ever. Sweat and copper made a nauseous combination, almost impossible to stand. Ivy tried hard not to breathe too often, to avoid the abhorrent odour.

The two boys were standing next to her. She had promised to bring them back, and she kept her word. Not that she could have left them by themselves. Her pay, which she had collected from that rotten bastard's office at the airharbour, exceeded her expectations. One more reason to do what Lady Hollingsworth had asked of her.

It was still hard to believe how suddenly her employer had turned from an elegant and prim lady into a wild cat climbing down an airship's folding ladder without a second thought. She was unlike other ladies she had encountered. So different that it made her wonder whether she really was an aristocrat.

She had heard of Rowena Hollingsworth, of how she changed the lives of many poor people in St. Giles, offering them a place to learn a craft. Everyone respected her so much that she could walk anywhere unchaperoned and nobody would judge her.

Perhaps, for such a person, a behaviour like she had witnessed earlier, undoubtedly still forbidden in their society, was acceptable.

The sudden shriek of the gondotram arriving at Blackfriars Bridge startled her.

"We're getting off soon," Ivy said, happy at the prospect of breathing like a human being again. "Be careful not to –"

But Erik and Blake had already sneaked out on the platform.

"'Scuse me, Miss aeronaut, but we can't go home just yet!" Erik yelled from the other side. "We must help 'er Ladyship!"

Ivy opened her mouth to say something, but the two boys were rushing down the metal stairs of the skystation, disappearing behind the closing doors of the wagon.

~

"JUDGING from the filthy state of your clothes, the chaos downstairs, and the utterly impossible stench of cheap alcohol in this room, I can only believe that allowing you to leave home and move here was one of my most astonishing mistakes."

Jasper didn't want to open his eyes. He hoped that voice was only the concoction of his hangover. That it would disappear once he was fully awake, and his brother was not a physical and tangible presence in his room.

Yet he was.

Edmund Asher, the Earl of Wyverstone, was standing in front of his bed.

"Wasn't the note enough?" Jasper asked, sitting up and rubbing the haze off his eyes. "Why did you come?" Still half asleep, he staggered in the general direction of the washbasin. If his brother's presence wasn't an illusion, he could at least face it awake and sober.

"I had to confirm you understood the meaning of my note. Which apparently you did not – since I saw it in your wastebasket."

"Good. Then you have my answer. Now leave. I am in no shape to receive guests."

"Do yourself a favour and live like a human, not like a wild animal." The uninvited visitor opened the windows, letting the air in.

"Edmund!" Jasper snapped. "I do not need you to air my bedroom or take care of its cleaning. Mrs Carraway is in charge of that. Now I cannot even sleep because you stormed my place! What the bloody hell do you want?"

"You must attend the customary dinner on Saturday," Edmund said, unbothered by Jasper's diatribe. "This year I shall not accept any infantile disregard of this request."

That was Edmund. Sharp as a knife, knowing where and when to cut for the most intense effect. Infantile disregard! Jasper felt his blood boiling but refrained from arguing. It would have been useless.

Besides, he didn't rule out the possibility that his brother had some ulterior motives to bring him back to the house he had left so long ago. On the very day he hated that house the most.

"And I suggest you clean your workshop. You will need it for more serious pursuits soon. Stop idling around, doing petty mechanical work. Your talents lie elsewhere."

Jasper stared at his brother in a futile attempt to read his face. The Earl of Wyverstone was only five years older than him, but they couldn't have been more different. Tall and impeccably dressed, his black hair neatly combed and his intense blue eyes impossible to decipher, Edmund was commanding without the slightest effort.

The nature of his work made him as unreadable as a stone. However, in time, Jasper came to understand at least some patterns of his behaviour and actions. He knew his older brother better than anyone.

Edmund's unexpected presence might mean more than he let him see. His brother would have never bothered to come there and complain about the state of his workshop without a good reason. Likewise, he wouldn't have forced him to attend a social event he loathed unless the importance of the matter required him to do so.

Downstairs, Jasper wiped a corner of his workbench with his forearm and poured tea into two old mismatched cups, realising he was no different from a barbarian in Edmund's eyes. For a man so obsessed with manners such as him, the way Jasper made the tea was close to heresy.

"What is the connection between Master Hollingsworth's trap in the Westminster Tower, my presence at that blasted dinner, and how I should use my workshop?" Jasper asked quickly, avoiding the impending disapproval of his lack of finesse. "I'm not patient enough for your riddles."

Edmund's features lightened in a smile that carved small dimples in his cheeks and made him look at least a few years younger than his twenty-seven years of age.

"Seeing that you can still use your brain gives me hope you are not yet lost." He sipped his tea, ignoring its unworthy container. "You must return. You had enough time to loiter around, but everything comes to an end.

"Theophilus Hollingsworth told you Her Majesty wants a new airship for the Engineers World Gathering. And the Marquess of Leythfordham is pulling some strings to be assigned as her chief engineer. But allowing that man to take charge would mean an unfathomable disaster.

"What happened three years ago must absolutely not repeat, so we need you back. *I* need you back. To your workbench, and into the service. I need your brain and skills for a mission of utmost importance."

Jasper's face darkened. He expected that, yet he suddenly remembered why he didn't like being around his brother.

He reminded him of a life he was trying hard to forget.

"No! I would rather fix clocks and pocket watches and make petty devices that will not bring any fame to my name. I do not care to know what you want from me. Find someone else."

"It is not you who decides whether you return," Edmund said, his hard and pointed voice leaving no place for disagreement. "It might be because of these three years you lived your life aimlessly among strangers, but you seem to forget who you are."

He looked straight at Jasper.

"I shall refresh your memory. You are an excellent engineer and an agent in Her Majesty's intelligence service. We appointed you as the engineer for the planned royal airship."

"My answer is still no. Working on Her Majesty's airship is the last thing I want to do."

Edmund went to one of the tall windows of the workshop, staring at the little street outside for a few long moments.

"We shall open an investigation for *The Golden Griffin*," he said, turning again to Jasper. "I agreed to oversee the new airship from the shadow if they handed me that case. Yesterday I received the official document of approval from the Royal House."

Jasper froze, finally understanding the real reason of his brother's visit.

"How?" he asked. "The Engineers Order will never accept this. They were quite adamant about dismissing the incident as an unforeseen technical failure. Handing you the case would mean admitting they were wrong."

"The Engineers Order is still under the authority of Her Majesty, no matter how much they want to believe otherwise. Yet, planning airships is under their control. This is why I want you in charge. I need to keep my eyes on the new airship project, while investigating the previous one – without any unnecessary interference from the Order."

"Benedict Quimby will not be too pleased to support me. I am no longer an active member, and he is backing Leythfordham."

"He agreed," Edmund said. "You will receive an official letter, but don't accept the proposal too willingly. I do not want him to suspect you know. I worked quite a bit to make him sign the transfer papers for *The Golden Griffin* case. He insisted on keeping the case closed to protect you, but he eventually conceded."

"Protect me?" Jasper didn't know whether to be amused or angry. "Protect me from what?"

"From a trial. You were in charge of the engine configuration of that airship. He is certain an investigation would bring you to the gaol for negligence in service. That is why the unforeseen technical failure verdict. Needless to say, I am now even more suspicious of the Order."

"Bollocks!" Jasper laughed at the unexpected revelation. "Ridiculous! The *Griffin* passed all the engine checks! I have nothing to hide!"

The front door flying open cut off Edmund's answer.

Blake and Erik Killen burst in, panting and red-faced.

"What are you doing here?" Jasper asked. "Did something happen to Jack?"

"No, Master Jasper," Erik said. "To 'er Ladyship! You must come!"

"You mean Rowena?" When both boys nodded, Jasper's features turned from worry to panic. "What happened to her?"

"We'll tell you, but hurry! It's the school!"

"ARE YOU CERTAIN THE BUILDING FELL?" Jasper asked the two boys who were struggling to match his stride. "Perhaps you misunderstood."

"Lady Rowena said so," Eric confirmed. "Then she climbed down the airship on a folding ladder!"

Despite her graceful demeanour, she was fearless. He had learnt that a long time ago, several months after Jade's death.

The night he had hurt her still burnt his memories.

He had been drinking at the Copper Kettle for hours, trying to obliterate any memory of *The Golden Griffin* and Jade. Leaving home and moving into his workshop near Blackfriars Bridge hadn't been enough. His nights were as tormented as when he lived in Grosvenor Crescent.

Oblivion came easier in that dirty pub. His senses could only distinguish burnt grease and smoke, cheap gin and sweat. The chatter and clatter around him had vanished into a distant buzz. The brazen doxy beside him craving for his attention was but a shapeless shadow.

If you are so eager to waste yourself in a squalid gin house, I shall not stop you. Edmund's words from their last meeting resonated in his mind. *But neither your misery nor your tantrums will bring Jade back. Nothing will. If living like a coward is what you wish, you are not my brother anymore.*

Edmund be damned.

In a few days, he would leave England. Embark on a ship and sail to Sydney. Go where no one knew him, and forget about Jade, Edmund, Rowena, and airships. The seas seemed more appealing than the skies lately.

"In about three months I shall be in Australia –"

"What Australia, lad! You can't even reach the door. Go home! You're as drunk as a boiled owl."

He recognised the voices of the Copper Kettle's regulars. That was Jack Killen. The scrawny man who would take any job to feed his family.

"I don't have a home."

"The lady who always comes for you thinks otherwise. She's 'ere again. Leave 'im, lady!" he shouted. "He's as boozed as a stone!"

"I'm not leaving without Jasper! Please, help me bring him to the carriage!"

Rowena's voice irked him. Why couldn't she leave him be?

"Does Master Hollingsworth know where you are?" he mumbled. "Or how you're embarrassing yourself? This ain't a place for respectable ladies. Are you not tired of chasing after me?"

"Jasper, I'm taking you home. You cannot stay here."

"Why is that?" He looked at her, making sure she didn't miss the mockery behind the drunken haze of his eyes. "Who are you to tell me where I can or cannot stay?"

He turned to take the wench next to him in his arms. "As you see, I'm busy."

He kissed the woman, trying not to be sick. She reeked of stale beer and tobacco, her hair emanated a strong odour of grease and cheap perfume.

Which he didn't need to inhale for too long. Rowena dragged him from the woman's arms and out of the establishment, avoiding the drunken lot around them. How her delicate frame found such strength, he never understood.

They stopped in front of the compass clock – the massive contraption he had made a few months before – which dominated Seven Dials. It was glowing with a russet tint in the crude light of the streetlamp.

"I remember your words when you first showed me this," she said, still holding him. "To help the lost ones find their way. You are lost, but I shall help you find your way."

"Rowena, you became such a bore! Leave and never come after me again!"

"You are too drunk to think straight." She gripped his hand tighter, dragging him closer. "I am not going anywhere without you."

"Leave me alone! I do not need you! Or Edmund! Rot in hell for all I care!"

He pushed her with such force that she crashed into the spherical structure's iron post. Her body slumping down at the base of the compass and the thin red strand of blood trickling down her cheek sobered him in an instant.

He had done something abhorrent and unforgivable.

"Rowe –" He pulled her to him, holding her tight. "I was a bloody idiot! Rowe, forgive me!"

"Stop squeezing me or I shall suffocate. Your shirt smells like the Thames during the Great Stink." Her voice was a muffled sound in the dirty fabric of his clothes.

Jasper freed her, gently wiping the blood off her face with the back of his hand. No matter how drunk he had been, he should have never hurt her.

"I miss you, Jasper. I do not want to lose you. Return to me, please. Do not push me away –"

She wrapped her arms around his neck, and he held her again. What was he doing? What madness had almost sent him to Australia on a ship when she needed him in that cursed city?

"I don't need this compass," he said, his voice a soft whisper against her ear. "If I am ever lost, my only north is you."

The merry whistling of the crowd in front of the Copper Kettle startled them. Rowena straightened herself up, but it was too late. Everyone had seen her in Jasper's arms.

That night, he had vowed to stay by her side no matter what.

"What a distasteful joke!" Rowena was trying to keep her composure, but the events were taking a toll on her. "What do you mean, closing my school?"

"I apologise, my lady, but these are the orders." Another constable handed her a paper. "As a result of this incident, you cannot open another school here. The decree has the seal of the Inspectorates."

Rowena read the paper twice, letting the meaning of his words sink in. Her school would disappear along with the building.

Or not.

She remembered *The Skycradle* and had another idea. If Ivy Blackwell agreed, she would reopen her charity.

"Yer Ladyship!" Erik and Blake made a triumphant appearance alongside Jasper.

Rowena turned to them, surprised and relieved. With Jasper's help, she could overcome anything. She took his arm and briefed him on the events of the day.

"This doesn't sit well with me," Jasper said, running his fingers through the tousled black strands of hair that covered his blue eyes. "Or maybe too many things have occurred today and I'm just going mad. I'm taking you home. I wouldn't let you go anywhere alone looking like that."

Only then Rowena noticed the loose locks of her hair, her dirty dress and boots, and her lost hat, and felt her cheeks burning. She nodded, and soon they were in the safe enclosure of a carriage.

"I cannot understand who would want to hurt you, but it is impossible for that building to fall like it did. Or for the Inspectorates to issue that decree so quickly, without investigating what happened. You should fill an inquiry."

"I know. Airships do not blast out of nowhere, and buildings do not fall out of nowhere – I only hope this time we shall learn the truth."

All strength drained from his muscles. The recollection of what the pain of loss felt like engulfed him with the force of a lightning storm.

Rowena could have been inside the school.

The thought almost choked him. If not for her airship trip, she could have been dead.

"Please, worry not," she said, sensing his dread. "I shall be all right."

But he was far from reassured.

4

Cleaning the workshop proved to be a much more painful undertaking than Jasper had thought. Pieces of metal, cables, gauges, and dials were spread in disarray all over the place. So much time had passed since he last created something that he had forgotten the original purpose for most of them.

Edmund was right, he thought with a pang in his chest. He kept idling around, doing nothing but fixing clocks and trinkets, in a daily routine of self-deception. Peace – he had it. Yet, while struggling to find a place on the shelves for those dismembered parts, he realised how he longed to give them a new identity.

If only that damned night never happened. The night when time stopped for him, when Jasper the airship engineer died, resurrecting as a petty mechanic content with a dull life amidst glasses of cheap gin at the Copper Kettle.

He had avoided a much worse fate – in an opium den or with a knife in his throat – but that wasn't much of a relief. Time had taught him how to suppress the memories, the thoughts which reminded him of his former self.

"I assume you became as tedious and sloppy as this place. Such a workshop is by no means worthy of a distinguished member of the Engineers Order. It is disgustingly dull, full of parts that would only make a clock for the servants' quarters."

Jasper would still recognise that thin and aggravating voice anywhere. He turned around, determined not to show the annoyance that said voice stirred in him. Too many unexpected guests kept appearing at his doorstep, but that one repulsed him the most. Alexis McQuillian, Marquess of Leythfordham, in his working space was a rather unpalatable image.

"To what do I owe the honour of such an illustrious visit?" Jasper asked, making sure the sarcasm reached as far as the docks near Blackfriars Bridge. "I cannot tend to guests, for I have work to do. It will take hours to finish, so I'm afraid I must see you out."

"Kind and welcoming as usual." The man's disapproving snort stirred in Jasper the desire to punch his small and pointy nose. "But I didn't come here expecting you to be either."

Jasper said nothing, hoping he would leave soon. He didn't trust Leythfordham, who fancied himself as an inventor without ever creating anything to bring him a name. Yet, the marquess aspired to be the next head of the Engineers Order – or the next royal mechanic following Theophilus Hollingsworth's retirement.

"I believe you are aware that the Engineers Order's Assembly is in two months." He moved closer to one of the tall iron-framed windows, where the natural light turned his blond hair almost white.

"Enough with this boring preamble. Why are you here?"

"To give you a sound piece of advice. Quit the Order. It's less shameful than being ousted."

"I don't recall the Board giving me a warning."

"Some engineers don't consider you worthy anymore. What have you done in the last three years? You didn't attend the assemblies, didn't *invent* anything, didn't *discover* anything. Only repaired clocks and devices for the poor of St. Giles. If it weren't for your brother and your family name, you would starve along with the destitute lot you are loitering with. Such behaviour is not appropriate for a member of our Order. I shall request your exclusion at the next assembly."

How mistaken Jasper had been to believe Leythfordham could not be more annoying than he remembered. The bony man in front of him had just reached another level of getting on his nerves, and the itch to punch his face only grew stronger.

The marquess' hatred towards him was no secret, as he had never bothered to hide his venom. Jasper had received the invitation into the Order when he was eighteen, while Leythfordham, almost ten years older than him, had used his name and money to secure a membership.

"It's remarkable how enlightened you are about what I do and who I'm loitering with," Jasper said. "My membership is not your concern. However, what you are planning to do in St. Giles is mine. As tedious and sloppy as I might be, you can bet on your name I shall not let you have it your way. Now leave. I am too busy sorting out parts for servant quarters' clocks."

"Oh, news travels fast." Leythfordham's feigned surprise irked Jasper. "I haven't imagined my *scientific plans* are so famous. A new airharbour would mean progress not only for the Engineers Order, but for those unfortunate paupers as well. How will you stop me? By the time we build it, your membership will be history.

"One more thing." The marquess stopped with one hand on the knob of the entrance door. "I hear the Inspectorates closed Lady Hollingsworth's charity. That woman should settle and pay more attention to her place in the civilised society instead of following you around among drunkards and whores. She needs a husband to tame her for good and knock some sense into her."

The punch Jasper had struggled to keep at bay claimed its way against the uninvited guest's face, with a power that made his neck turn onto the designated trajectory of the blow.

"Likes of you should not roam freely among good people!" The marquess threw Jasper a poisonous look while wiping out the thin thread of blood coming out of his nose. "I'll make sure you rot in hell!"

Jasper opened the door and hurled him out without answering. He was well aware that, if he didn't disappear from his sight, he would beat him senseless.

IVY STARED at the Hollingsworth mansion reluctantly, holding the embossed name card. The only connection she ever had with the upper class was as an aviator flying her aristocratic customers in leisure trips over London or to the countryside. That world was closed to her, and she could count on one hand the times she had called on such a family.

Rowena Hollingsworth's servant bringing her the invitation card had been a surprise. Perhaps she wanted to thank her personally for the day before? Or to reprimand her for how the two brats had fooled her?

A thousand possibilities went through her head while searching for a bell string or a door knocker. Seeing nothing but a small button mounted next to the door, Ivy assumed it was the only way in, and pressed it.

She adjusted the bonnet that tamed her wavy red hair and smoothed the folds of her long green dress. The outfit was nowhere near comfortable, but she couldn't stroll through Mayfair in her worn-out aeronaut gear. After a considerable amount of effort, Eudora had turned her into a somewhat presentable young woman.

At least when it came to her outer appearance.

A steammotor stopped in front of the house. The driver removed his cap and goggles, revealing a tangle of blond hair, and strode to her.

What a weird man. Why wear an aviator cap when driving a vehicle?

Then she noticed it had covered a swollen and bruised cheek. But the newcomer didn't have the chance to greet her or introduce himself. The door opened, and the butler welcomed them into the mansion.

"Miss Blackwell, Her Ladyship is waiting for you. Your Lordship, I shall accompany you to Master Hollingsworth's study."

The weird man threw her a startled look when he heard her name, but she didn't pay too much attention to him. He took the stairs, while she followed the maid to the drawing room.

A light knock announced the guest, and Rowena invited her in.

The room was cosy and elegant without being lavish. On a mahogany desk near the French doors facing the garden, papers piled up on an open ledger next to a brass typewriter.

Lady Hollingsworth smiled, beckoning her to sit. She

pressed her finger on a small button similar to the one at the entrance door. A maid came in shortly after, bringing tea and scones.

"Miss Blackwell, thank you so much for accepting my invitation," Rowena said. "I shall explain why I need you and *The Skycradle*."

She sat on the armchair opposite Ivy's and took one of the two cups on the tray.

"I had a school, a charity for the people in St. Giles, to help them learn a craft and seek better employment opportunities. But now my school is a heap of bricks and broken furniture. There is no purpose left for a pile of rubble."

Ivy still failed to understand where she and her airship fit in the story. "You can always move it to another building, I assume?"

"No, I cannot. The Inspectorates came to some erroneous conclusions and would not allow me to open another school there. Those people need my charity, so I thought that if a building wouldn't do, *The Skycradle* would."

"You mean turning it into a school? My airship?"

"Yes. I shall rent your services for that. Does it make any difference whether you fly for sightseeing or educational purposes?"

She had a point, Ivy admitted. Besides, the strange proposal was an unexpected income source for her when she most needed one. Lady Hollingsworth was right. She didn't care what her passengers talked about or what they did – as long as they didn't damage her craft. She saw no reason to turn her down.

"No. It makes no difference. I accept your offer."

Rowena slumped into her armchair, glad she didn't need to play the perfect host anymore. Her plan went well, but the last few days had drained her.

That was not her favourite time of the year either. The fragrance of the garden in early summer filled the room through the open windows. Yet, in her mind, it was entwined with the sour odour of sorrow and loss. It reminded her of a night three years before, when she inhaled the same scent.

The night Jade Kendall Asher died.

The sound of the door opening made her turn in time to see Theophilus Hollingsworth entering the drawing room, an unusual appearance that time of day. With his back slightly crooked, his white shoulder-length hair thinner by the day, and the blurry pince-nez stuck on his nose, he seemed much older and worn.

"Father, why are you home this early? Is anything the matter?"

"Nothing of importance," he said, dismissing her question. "I had to receive the Marquess of Leythfordham – we had some matters to discuss. But now it is you I want to talk about." He settled comfortably in an armchair, looking straight at her. "Are you attending the Earl of Wyverstone's dinner tomorrow?"

She met his gaze with a sorrowful look. "Yes, I must do so."

"My dear child, you need to move on," her father said. "It is unfortunate, but Jade cannot return from the dead. Both you and Jasper need to start from where you left three years ago.

"Perhaps you should take it as a sign. What happened to your school, I mean. Think of your happiness. You have done so much for those people, and things are changing quickly. Perhaps they do not need you anymore."

Rowena stared at him, too startled to think of an answer right away. He had always supported her work, knowing what the school meant to her. She wanted to thank those people, who had helped her drag Jasper out of his misery after his brother's death, when he was spending his days getting drunk, picking fights, and giving up on himself.

She rested her hand on her father's bony fingers. "I'm happy at the school. I need those people as much as they need me. I cannot abandon them. Jasper is happy in his own way. I can tell you that. The Order might be disappointed, but he still needs time. Worry not, sooner or later he will be back to his workbench."

"It's complicated," Theophilus Hollingsworth said. "The Order is not that patient, and they have been waiting for quite a long time. Doing nothing for three years when you are a member of the most important Order in England is unacceptable. All the more when we are talking about such raw talent as Jasper's. Some voices are talking about his exclusion and Leythfordham's promotion as Secretary. It would be a disaster for the boy."

"The only people he ever listens to are you and the Earl of Wyverstone." Rowena stood up and started pacing around the room. "I hoped they would understand and wait for him. I urge you to talk to him. What would become of the Order if Leythfordham gets promoted and Jasper excluded? For the love of God, this cannot happen!"

Crouched in his armchair, Theophilus Hollingsworth looked small and tired. Deep wrinkles riddled his face, and his hazy eyes were distant behind the dirty lenses. He worked less and less, and wished to pass on his legacy to Jasper, who still kept his distance from the world he used to love so much.

"You are right, my child. It cannot happen. And it will not."

~

JASPER STOPPED in front of the massive three-storey building which hosted all the Orders, the constabulary, the Office of Classified Affairs, the Navy, and all the other regulatory institutions reunited under the common name of the Inspectorates – the supreme ruling authority in England alongside the Royal House.

Almost a year had passed since he had last been there. But his brother's news and Leythfordham's visit were enough to make him close his workshop and find out what was going on, even without the official letter he had yet to receive.

He had taken his membership for granted, and that proved to be a mistake.

The first floor was an endless display of people going in and out of the Orders' offices – a buzz he used to love, and which he was pleased to rediscover.

"Jasper! How wonderful to see you here! You haven't called on us for *ages*! I keep telling Edmund you forgot the way to your own house!"

His older brother's wife was the last person he had expected to see coming out of the office he was about to enter.

"Emmeline, *my* house is on Tallis Street near Blackfriars, and I assure you I remember where I live." He didn't like her sly insinuation. She knew too well he had long ceased to consider the Wyverstone mansion in Grosvenor Crescent his home. "And you coming out of that office is more surprising than my presence here. As far as I recall, I am still a member."

"Oh, I only took a small detour to pay my respects to Mr Quimby. Of course, I am here for my husband."

She offered him her best smile and a little curtsey, then

disappeared in the crowd. Her visit was unusual, but, given Emmeline's obsession for appearances, he didn't think too much of it.

"You are the most unexpected guest of the day, and one I have been thinking of recently," Benedict Quimby – Senior Lord of the Engineers Order – said with his usual affable smile when he entered his office. "I am most curious to find out what brings you here."

Jasper sat in the leather armchair across from Quimby. "I caught wind of some distressing news which I wanted to confirm with you. Is it true that the Order will appoint the Marquess of Leythfordham as the airship engineer of the Royal House's project for the Gathering?"

"As you might know, I have someone else in mind." The Senior Lord squinted at him with a meaningful look. "You must return to your duties. Otherwise, you will lose all support within the Order. The Board is now assessing the Marquess of Leythfordham's idea. However, if you can guarantee your full commitment, I shall give this assignment to you."

"I cannot offer such guarantees, for my long absence makes me unworthy of such a task. I also understand the Board intends to exclude me from the Order."

"Nonsense! I shall not tolerate any argument on that matter. You are a member of the Engineers Order, and this will not change. I have a few ways to appease Leythfordham – should he insist on your exclusion."

"Such as?"

"Do not concern yourself with that. I shall keep the marquess content enough to keep his mouth shut."

"If keeping him content means granting him permission to build a private airharbour in St. Giles, I would rather have him displeased."

"Jasper, he only wants the area around the former rookery. It is hard to refuse him both requests. He is one of the main sponsors of the Order, and we owe a lot to his father." Benedict Quimby stood up, his hands clasped behind his back. "He has the support of some of the most powerful noble families in England. Do not forget Lady Emmeline Asher and her brother are his friends. Of course, you are aware that the Duke of Herdforthbridge is the second most important nobleman after the members of the Royal House."

That explains Emmeline's presence at the Inspectorates! Jasper thought. *It was not to see Edmund, but to speak up for Leythfordham! The Duke of Herdforthbridge's loathing towards the Engineers Order is well known. He would never come here himself! He sent his sister instead!*

"I do not agree with his plans," Benedict Quimby said. "But I prefer to let him have that airharbour rather than appoint him as the chief engineer for Her Majesty's airship. Since I first received the notice, I only had you in mind. For such a project, the most suitable – no, the *only* choice is you, Jasper. No one would object or still support the marquess if the alternative is you."

"I shall think about that." Jasper stared at the intricate patterns of the walnut desk. "You are right. It is time I returned into the Order."

~

"THEN I SHALL SEE you tomorrow night. Jasper's presence and my announcement will surprise everyone. Oscar, I am counting on your excellent observation abilities. I need a proper assessment of their reactions."

Edmund put the speakerbox receiver into its brass hook just as his wife entered the office.

"Emmeline, this is your third visit in one week. Need I remind you that you cannot come here as you please?"

"Oh, I hoped you would join me for lunch. I cannot recall the last time we dined together! Your work always keeps you busy here, while I am always feeling lonely in that house."

That house was his ancestral home. She had a particular talent to irk him with such remarks, which he decided to ignore.

"You would not guess who I met here earlier," she said when they were out of the Inspectorates building. "Your brother. What a surprise to find him at Benedict Quimby's door. Has he remembered he still is a member of the Engineers Order, perhaps?"

"I am not acquainted with Jasper's plans. He is free to do whatever he wishes."

"You are too lenient with such an ungrateful spoiled rascal! Three years ago, he left home as a drunkard to live among beggars. He did not care he disgraced his family and destroyed Lady Hollingsworth's reputation. What respectable woman rambled in gin bars to drag out a pariah? No wonder no decent gentleman is now interested in marrying her."

Edmund stopped, prompting her to look at him. No matter how hard he tried to tolerate her, they always ended up in disagreement.

"My dear, talking about my brother in that manner or about what he used to do three years ago does not fit my idea of having lunch. I'm afraid I lost my appetite."

His voice was sharp enough to make his intentions clear.

"You would not discard me in the middle of the street."

"No, I would not. I shall take you to your carriage. Have dinner without me tonight. I must work until late."

Emmeline's practised smile never left her face as he changed direction to return to the Inspectorates. A chilly wind was ruffling the ribbons of her bonnet and the blonde curls of her hair. She squeezed his arm tighter, and Edmund inhaled the subtle floral fragrance of her violet perfume that matched her delicate petite figure so well. She was so beautiful, but it didn't matter. He could never fall for the person she was.

She might not be the most tolerable person, but at least try to understand her.

As much as he wanted to fulfil her brother's request, he found it impossible to do so.

He looked up at the suspended mobile pathway that followed the fringe of St. James Park. Regardless of the wind and the cloudy sky, the crowds still filled the place. The metallic promenade was circling the entire park in a slow movement, carrying couples smiling at each other, children leaning over the railing, young ladies with their chaperones.

An image of casual happiness whose taste he had long forgotten.

"Your Lordship, Your Ladyship –" The coachman's hoarse voice made Edmund realise they had arrived at the carriage. "If I may, I found this under the vehicle's door. I thought I should give it to you. Looked important."

Edmund took the small object – a thick ring engraved with a cogwheel and the initials of the Engineers Order.

"You did well," Edmund said, noticing how Emmeline's face turned paler. "Now leave us and prepare to take Her Ladyship home.

"Emmeline, I am most curious to understand why this ring was under your carriage. Only a few members of the Order own this seal, so I presume they are careful enough not to lose it."

"I must have dropped it there. I found it a few days ago on

the steps as I was leaving the Inspectorates. Today I wanted to give it to Benedict Quimby but could not find it anywhere."

"I shall return it to him. You should have told me about this."

"Oh, how could I have bothered the Chief Inspector of Her Majesty's Office of Classified Affairs with such a trifle!" Emmeline's smile had returned, as mocking as ever. She let go of his arm to step into her carriage.

Only that finding an Engineers Order seal ring on the steps of the Inspectorates was highly unlikely – and far from a trifle.

~

Late in the afternoon, Ivy was hurrying back to the airharbour, after a detour home to change into her aeronaut gear. She had just landed a contract, weird as it was, and she wanted to make sure everything was in place, and *The Skycradle* was ready. It was an odd one, but still a contract that would bring her some financial stability, at least for a while.

"Miss Blackwell," the airharbour gatekeeper said, "Mr Hayes was asking for you a few minutes ago. You should go to the office."

Ivy changed directions, turning towards the red building of the Airharbour Assignments Office. Maybe he had another contract for her? Could she be that lucky? Or, on the contrary, something happened to her ship?

She found the clerk at his desk in his stuffy little room, but he wasn't alone. His guest was a dark-haired man in his late twenties, handsome yet intimidating. His blue eyes were as sharp as a blade, and only when he stood she realised how tall and commanding he was. Judging from his expensive fine clothes, and from his bearing, she guessed he was a nobleman.

"Good afternoon, Miss Blackwell." Hayes was talking in a mellow tone he never used with her. "Please allow me to introduce His Lordship Edmund Asher, the Earl of Wyverstone – one of Her Majesty's most trusted officers at the Inspectorates."

Edmund graced her with a perfectly executed bow, which Ivy returned in a much less graceful manner, wondering what an officer from the Inspectorates would want from her.

"I'm honoured to make your acquaintance." The intimidating guest finally spoke, his deep rich voice making him even more imposing. "I would like to apologise beforehand for a request that might sound rude to Miss Blackwell," he said, turning to Hayes. "I need to discuss some confidential matters with her. So, I would like to ask you to leave us for a few minutes."

Then he addressed Ivy again.

"Miss Blackwell, I assure you of my complete regard, so please do not be offended. Had it not been for the nature of this matter, I would not have dared to ask for such a thing."

Not only handsome and elegant but also a manners maniac, Ivy thought, not sure whether to laugh or be annoyed.

"I shall get straight to the point," the earl said, after Hayes left the office. "You own something I am extremely interested in purchasing. I am ready to make an offer worth of such an item."

"What such an item would be?" Ivy asked, with a sinking feeling in her chest.

"The plans of Octavia and Chalford Blackwell's last airship prototype."

So, the day she had dreaded finally arrived. The day when

someone would come for her and her precious legacy, the most important thing she had from her parents.

"What if I don't have them?" she tried, but her tone betrayed her and the Earl of Wyverstone was not one to be fooled.

"That would have been a terrible loss," he replied without batting an eye. "But, as it appears, we are fortunate enough to have avoided such damage, since they are in your care."

"Why are you so certain? I lived in another country, and my parents never shared their work with me. How could they trust me with such important documents? That's absurd!"

"Miss Blackwell, I mean no harm. If I did, those papers would have already been in my hands – I can assure you of that. I only want to propose a mutually beneficial deal. Of course, I understand it would be most unwise of you to trust a stranger with something as important as your parents' work. You need to be sure I am telling the truth, so I shall give you that proof. Three years ago, in Paris, Octavia and Chalford Blackwell gave you those documents in a brown leather cylinder case with a tattered lid. Two weeks before *The Golden Griffin* incident. Am I right?"

"I don't understand how you know that detail, but they are not for sale. You are wasting your time," Ivy said, aware of how rude she was. "I want to make that airship myself. One day. When I have enough money and time and experience and resources. I don't want them in the hands of a stranger or the Aviators Order."

"I have considered this possibility," the earl said, undeterred by her refusal. "Which is why when I said I wanted to purchase your parents' airship plans I meant something else.

"You studied in Paris, and you are an excellent airship mechanic." He kept talking, encouraged by Ivy's silent gaze.

"What would you say if I gave you the chance to work on this very project? To see that airship come to life? Rest assured, I have the power to make sure both you and your documents will be out of harm's way. I shall explain all the details in a moment."

She stared at him in disbelief, unsure of what to make of his words. Was he a lunatic who came there to mock her? Or an imposter who wanted to trick her into giving him her most treasured possession? But only a few people had seen the leather case where her parents kept those plans, so he couldn't be a liar.

"I would happily accept such an offer. But why would I trust your words? How can I be sure you are not like all the others who tried to steal those papers from me?"

"Miss Blackwell, we want to use your parents' plans for Her Majesty's new airship. If you agree, we shall present it at the Engineers World Gathering next spring. If you refuse, I shall leave you alone. I have no intention to steal anything from you."

"I understand. However, I'm not sure if I'll be able to do it all by myself. I know the theory, but I never actually designed an airship."

"Worry not. You will work with one of the best members the Engineers Order has ever had."

5

At sunset, Jasper got off at Victoria Station, the last barrier between Belgravia and the noisy London of gondotrams, tube, and trains. The place was quiet, but he didn't find that odd. The only extravagances the neighbourhood allowed were the mechanical horses and the steammotors, which had replaced the private carriages almost entirely.

He walked to his old home in Grosvenor Crescent with little enthusiasm. For two years, he had avoided the dinner Edmund organised in Jade's remembrance. Not even their own mother attended, so why should he? He had enough to carry on his shoulders without being reminded of that dreadful night in such a manner.

Had he not pushed Jade, had he not switched places with him, his twin brother would have been still alive. But the Queen had promised promotion for the entire crew. Taking part in that damned test flight would have made Jade a first rank officer in Her Majesty's service, changing his frivolous way of life.

Jasper wanted to help him, only to send him to his death. The airship had turned into an enormous ball of fire in the sky, until nothing but cinders remained. He still couldn't understand how such a craft could blast like that. Even worse, everyone turned a deaf ear when he desperately sought to find out the truth. His judgement told him the ship had been rigged, but, apart from Edmund, nobody listened.

When he arrived at the mansion, his mind was still lost in memories. His brother's butler saw him to the drawing room, where the surprised looks of the guests indicated that his presence was unexpected.

Lady Emmeline Rexworth Asher quickly hid her astonishment behind a perfect smile glued on her pale face framed by blonde curls. Her simple dark crimson gown favoured her small and slim figure, with a black velvet choker as her only embellishment.

The Countess of Wyverstone fully deserved her fame as one of the most beautiful women in London.

"How thoughtful of you to join us!" she said, without the slightest hint at their meeting the previous day at the Inspectorates. "It is a remarkable, and no less pleasant surprise to see you here."

Jasper bowed, kissing her hand. "Emmeline, I am glad to find you in good health."

He greeted the others, before going to Rowena and Theophilus Hollingsworth. The Marquess of Leythfordham's cheek was still swollen, but it served him right. Oscar Bashford – Emmeline's brother and the Duke of Herdforthbridge – looked as bored as ever. The duke and Edmund had been colleagues at Eton, but they were too different to be close. Surely, his presence was only a matter of etiquette.

"We were talking about what happened to Lady Hollingsworth's school," Emmeline said. She smoothed the folds of her dress after retaking her seat next to Edmund, her eyes on Rowena. "I cannot understand how such a thing occurred. Perhaps it is time you left those slums behind. Find a husband, settle down, and take care of Master Hollingsworth. Provided that he will soon leave Her Majesty's service, of course."

The flicker in Edmund's eyes was the only evidence of his anger, but Jasper didn't miss it. Emmeline's impertinence was nothing new to him. She always believed her social status allowed her liberties Edmund would never tolerate. It was only one of the many things that made her so different from the Earl of Wyverstone.

"Thank you for being so considerate," Rowena said, with a faint gleam of disbelief in her eyes. "I have decided to pursue my activities, nonetheless. I found another place for my school. A rather unusual one. But will do."

"I am not planning to retire any time soon," Theophilus Hollingsworth said. "If this is my daughter's wish, I choose to trust her. Even when it means hosting her school in an airship."

"An *airship*? Teaching while flying over London? How did you find a navigator who agreed to this unladylike madness?" Emmeline's bewilderment was genuine.

"A brilliant idea!" Edmund said, without looking at his wife. "The authorities will leave you alone, since you are only taking your passengers on educational trips. No one would dare say anything, given your reputation. Lady Hollingsworth, allow me to congratulate you for your clever choice."

"Rowena, dear, you are truly your father's daughter!" A

good-natured smile brightened Benedict Quimby's plump face. "Contracting an airship for your charity pursuits is commendable. Remind your critics we live in an era that favours technology and evolution."

"Worry not," Rowena replied. "I would never give anyone any reason to talk. My navigator is a woman. Quite a competent one, as I had the occasion to witness myself."

"A woman navigator?" Emmeline's brother asked contemptuously. "Her Majesty is much too permissive with her idea of progress. Letting women fly airships and allowing them into the Royal Orders. I wonder what comes next."

"On the contrary, Herdforthbridge," Quimby said, squinting at him. "Her Majesty is much too permissive with the old ways. She rejected some brilliant inventions our Order wanted to implement. Our country lost so much! The Queen has yet to understand that her ancient sense of ethics compromises advancement."

"Quimby, do not speak treason!" The duke's eyes flickered, as sharp as steel. "You might be the Senior Lord of the Engineers Order, but you are still Her Majesty's subject!"

"Gentlemen, please do not digress. We have a more interesting matter to talk about," the Marquess of Leythfordham said, with the asinine look Jasper despised so much. "Lady Hollingsworth, Her Ladyship the countess is right about your marriage. What a pity for a beautiful and intelligent woman such as you not to think of her domestic happiness."

"How about minding *your* domestic happiness, Marquess?" Jasper didn't try to hide the irony in his voice. If these people wanted insolence, he would offer plenty of it. The deplorable spectacle thrown by the countess and her entourage was too much, and he couldn't stand to see

Rowena exposed to it any longer. "I cannot help noticing your concern about other people's affairs. If Lady Hollingsworth decides to marry, you will certainly receive an invitation to the ceremony."

~

JASPER MENTALLY THANKED his brother for placing him at the table in the farthest corner from the Marquess of Leythfordham. It had been a mistake to come, and he was more certain of that with every moment that passed. While Edmund coped admirably with his wife's arrogance, Jasper could never deal with it.

He still remembered Edmund's wedding, less than one month before Jade's death, after the shortest courtship in London's recent history. An event important enough to make the entire *ton* forget about the biggest scandal of that year, when the Duke of Herdforthbridge was abandoned at the altar by his fiancée who had fled to Australia in search of adventure.

Edmund and Emmeline had been the talk of all salons, and a sight to behold. The sister of one of the most powerful men in England was marrying the Chief Inspector of Her Majesty's Office of Classified Affairs. Everyone saw them as a match made in heaven, but Jasper still couldn't fathom Edmund's reasons for his marriage. Their mother had always favoured that union, but Edmund was not the man to marry whoever he was told to.

Emmeline was everything his older brother despised, yet he still kept the pretence of the perfect household. With a wife whom he did not love, and without an heir even after three years of marriage.

“Thank you all for coming.” Edmund stood up, his face as unreadable as always. “We gathered here tonight to honour the memory of our late brother Jade Kendall Asher and of those who died on *The Golden Griffin* three years ago. May their souls rest in peace.”

“May the Almighty rest their souls,” the marquess said. “What a regrettable loss, to be deprived of such great minds and hearts. We are fortunate Jasper is still with us. A blessing for us, and the Engineers Order. I shall drink to that.”

Jasper felt nauseous but pretended not to notice Leythfordham’s subtle mockery.

“What a wonderful idea!” Emmeline stood as well, her gaze on her brother-in-law. “We should honour the memory of the dear ones who left us, but also celebrate life. We lost Jade, but we should be grateful we still have Jasper. Don’t you agree, Edmund?”

On the outside, it was a very considerate toast, but Jasper was aware of Emmeline’s hatred towards him. Not only because he understood the actual state of Edmund’s marriage, but also because she supported the Marquess of Leythfordham within the Engineers Order. Jade, blissfully oblivious of Edmund’s household and with no interest in the Order, had not been a threat to her and the marquess. A good reason they preferred it had been Jasper in his stead on *The Golden Griffin*.

“My dear Emmeline, then my announcement will most certainly please you.” Edmund’s voice could freeze the Thames in an instant. “Since you are so happy Jasper is alive, you will rejoice to hear he will soon return to his workbench. Her Majesty and the Order have chosen him as the chief engineer of the new airship the Royal House wants for the Engineers World Gathering.”

So, the real reason for the dinner was his brother's announcement. Jasper was almost amused.

"What?!" Leythfordham stared at the Earl of Wyverstone, so dumbfounded he almost took the wrong cutlery for the *fillet de boeuf*. "With all due respect, but has the Royal House forgotten what happened to *The Golden Griffin*? That airship *exploded.* We lost her along with the entire crew. Shall we remember *who* worked on the engine configuration?"

"Please, let's not bring up that awful memory," Emmeline said with feigned indignation. "We are all prone to mistakes, especially when we are young. It was a most thoughtful gift from Her Majesty to our Jasper. He deserves a second chance."

Jasper looked at his brother. Edmund's dark blue eyes seemed to throw daggers. Regardless of his obsession for manners, his anger had become almost uncontrollable.

"Emmeline, a lady should refrain from talking such nonsense." Herdforthbridge, who had been focused solely on the entrées, with a blatant lack of interest in the heated debate unfolding around him, finally interfered. "Also, refrain from talking about things you do not know. It is a most unpleasant sight."

"Pardon me, Your Ladyship," Theophilus Hollingsworth said, "but I need to remind everyone that we still don't know what truly happened. I can bear witness to Her Majesty's high regard for Jasper. She never considered him at fault for *The Golden Griffin's* unfortunate fate."

"That is right, Jasper." Benedict Quimby avoided the astonished glare of the marquess. "Her Majesty trusts you, and so does the Order. We received no proposal worthy enough to represent our nation at the Engineers World Gathering. You must accept this assignment. Your talent is unparalleled."

"If not for us," Rowena said, "then do it for Jade. Remember how he was always so proud of you."

"We shall expect you to present the completed airship plan in two months, at the next assembly of the Engineers Order," Quimby said. "I signed the nomination paper. The Board will validate your proposal, and give the final approval, as customary."

"Thank you for showing me such trust," Jasper replied with a new determination, the last trace of doubt gone. Emmeline's insolence and the marquess' hate only incensed him to come to a decision avoided for far too long. "I accept to return in Her Majesty's service as a member of the Engineers Order. I hope I shall fulfil your expectations."

EDMUND'S PRIVATE STUDY, which he only used for his classified work, had always been Jasper's favourite place in the mansion.

He inhaled the scent of old books and leather so familiar to him, realising how he missed that small haven where he felt so comfortable.

"What is this all about?" he asked, relieved to be alone with his brother and talk openly. "You have more to tell me, ain't it so?"

He took the brandy Edmund offered him and installed himself in one of the upholstered chairs. His brother leaned on the iron frame of the glass wall overlooking the garden, across from him.

In the raw light of the room, the earl was as tall and unmovable as the statue of an Olympian god, his high cheekbones contrasting with the lean features of his face. They both had the blue eyes and raven hair of their mother, but that was where their similarities ended. Edmund always inspired awe and fear, even more than their late father.

"I need you to keep an eye on some people," Edmund said. "Have them watched, then report everything to me. I also need you to protect someone. But make sure she will never realise what you are doing."

"It looks like you will keep me rather busy." The younger brother grinned. The evening was turning unexpectedly interesting. "Who do you want me to watch?"

"The Marquess of Leythfordham and Emmeline. I want to know where they go, who they meet, where, and why. Everything."

"Are you asking me to tail your wife?" Jasper laughed incredulously. "Why on earth would you want me to spy on Emmeline? She is not my favourite person, but, apart from her venomous tongue, she doesn't quite qualify as a threat. Don't tell me you suspect she is cheating on you with the marquess."

"Be sure I would never tail her for a matter of no interest to me. Jasper, I have some things to tell you."

Edmund crossed the room to open the drawer of his desk and retrieve a sheet of paper. Jasper took it, recognising the handwriting.

"This is Carmina's last report on Herdforthbridge. Emmeline's brother never liked how the Royal House accepted the gondotram tracks, the airships, and everything else coming from the realm of science. He thinks such things are vulgar and undignified for London, and that the aristocracy should go on with the old ways. If it were up to him, we would still drive only carriages with real horses, and people would crowd in omnibuses.

"He was aghast to hear Her Majesty wanted an airship for the Royal House and tried to stop her. But the Queen didn't bend. Given all this, three years ago, Carmina assumed he was involved in a sedition case, against both the Royal House, and the Engineers Order. It was too obvious to be true, but I could not dismiss the possibility. Marrying his sister offered me a chance to find out. Of course, according to the general opinion, I just fulfilled Mother's wish."

"You married Emmeline just to keep an eye on the duke?" Jasper asked, astonished. His brother's notion of duty was almost absolute, but he never thought Edmund would go that far. "Did you have any idea what you were getting yourself into? You got stuck for the rest of your life with a woman you never wanted."

"I did not call you here to discuss my private matters," Edmund said, with an icy gaze. "I am certain now the duke had no connection to *The Golden Griffin*. While not a supporter of the Orders, he is a man of honour. However, you were right. The airship was rigged. Carmina thought she would reveal a plot if she exposed the duke. But it was too dangerous to let her continue.

"I had to do it myself. This is why I took her off that mission and married the duke's sister. Only that the duke was not involved, and I realised too late I was following the wrong lead. You know the rest. *The Griffin* turned to ashes. My plan to use Emmeline to get to the core of a plot failed. The Engineers Order closed the case, and my hands were tied. Fortunately, we can resume the investigation from where I left three years ago. Now Leythfordham wants a private airharbour, and my wife comes to the Inspectorates suspiciously often."

"Why didn't you tell me?" Jasper glared at his brother, with a sudden urge to be sick. "You had a lead all this time and never told anyone?"

"I did not tell you because you were a liability, putting

your heart ahead of your brain and too busy wasting yourself in the slums. Besides, I had no evidence, and you would have acted blindly. Now I have convinced Her Majesty that the Royal House of England needs to present a new airship at the Gathering next year, and she wants you to be in charge.

"Let us wait for Leythfordham and Emmeline to make a move. I would tail my wife myself, but I do not want her to suspect anything. Especially not after I found that seal ring of the Engineers Order under her carriage. I let her believe I fell for her blatant lie about finding it on the steps of the Inspectorates."

"Then I shall do as you say. I swear I shall avenge Jade's death, no matter the price." Jasper's eyes looked dark and menacing. "Now tell me the other thing. Who do you want me to protect?"

"Octavia and Chalford Blackwell's daughter, Ivy. She has the plans of her parents' last airship prototype. You will work together and use them for the new one. You understand how important those plans are. This second mission of yours might relate to the first.

"What happened to *The Golden Griffin* might be connected to the Blackwells' research in Scotland. But those two were never too clear about their work." He paused for another sip of brandy. "They guarded it strictly. I went there once to ask if they needed our protection, and Emmeline insisted on joining me. I doubt she travelled to that forsaken place out of passion for me. There are far too many questions left unanswered. And a lot of work for us to do."

Jasper sighed. He'd been unaware of all the things happening right before Jade's death, and later after that, while he was drowning in his own misery. Edmund had taken it all upon himself, trying to protect his agents. But he had failed and got stuck with Emmeline for a lifetime in the process. He realised the weight his brother carried on his shoulders.

Jasper knew that, once he left that room, there would be no turning back. That he would resume a life long forgotten.

But, strangely, he was looking forward to it.

6

For Jasper, the best moment to visit the Cinnamon Dove was in broad daylight. The girls were sleeping, and the place was quiet enough for him to have tea with Madame without any disturbances. He doubted she would receive him with open arms after such a long absence but had to try if he wanted his old team back.

"Master Asher!" the doorman said with a baffled look. "You are here for Madame, ain't it so? She's in the heating room. The boiler went bonkers, and she's downstairs to put it back 'erself. You know 'ow she is. Better taking care of things on 'er own."

Jasper gaped in surprise. He took the stairs to the heating room, where a multitude of wrenches, screws, wheels, and lifeless gauges were spread in disarray on the floor. The boiler in the corner seemed a dysfunctional copper monster, with parts missing and pipes coming out of its body like immense arms drilling into the walls.

"Carmina Harcourt, what in the devil's name are you doing?" he asked, half amused, and half exasperated. "Do you intend to devastate this poor machine completely?"

A head embellished with curls dyed in dark purple and gathered up in a loose chignon turned to him, revealing a startled face with bright green eyes. Four small earrings pierced the upper part of her right ear, and the silver locket he never saw her without was still around her neck.

Half of the scarlet butterfly tattoo on her collarbone was peeking above the neckline of her white chemise underneath the leather corset. The woman hadn't changed one bit. She was in her late twenties, and as beautiful and full of secrets as he recalled.

"Oh, my – Hello, Jasper." Carmina raised an eyebrow, with an undefined expression of sarcasm or surprise. She wiped her forehead with the back of her hand, smearing her complexion in the process.

"This beast broke, and the Cinnamon Dove without hot water is unthinkable. Since I was in a bit of a hurry, I tried my skills in mechanics. I dismantled it, so I expect a bit of praise for that."

Jasper laughed wholeheartedly. She was the same Carmina he remembered, different from any other Madame in London. Barefoot, in her brown leather corset and skirt studded with buckles and pockets, she looked like the owner of a workshop rather than of a pleasure den.

"How about letting me check? Without intending any disregard towards your skills, I believe it's a better idea. Why didn't you call for me? Not only now, but whenever you needed me."

"Oh, and you would have come running from the gin bar where you were forgetting about the entire world? Besides, asking for help is not something I usually do." A shadow covered her face for a fleeting moment. "Speaking of help, I am dead curious to know what brings you here. Don't tell me you felt a sudden urge to see me after two bloody years."

He kneeled next to her among wrenches and gauges. "Blimey, Carmina! You cannot spare me, can you? I shall fix this blasted boiler, then tell you over a cup of tea. Is that all right?"

"Provided that you'll teach me how to patch this metal bastard. I might need to do this again."

A while and a fixed boiler later, they were drinking tea in Carmina's private study – her small corner full of oddities, from compasses to earth globes, old books, and detailed maps affixed to the wooden panelling of the walls.

She took her usual seat in the leather armchair beside the tall window.

"Tell me what you want from me, but keep in mind one thing. If this involves that damned brother of yours, you'd better leave this instant. He's the last person I want to work with or meet."

"It *does* involve Edmund." Jasper couldn't lie to her, no matter what the truth would cost him. "But you will not meet him. I need your help. What do you have on the Marquess of Leythfordham?"

"Not too much. I don't waste my time on such poor imbeciles. What happened?"

"Nothing worth of consideration. Except that he wants to tear down the former rookery in St. Giles to build a private airharbour. Now he is gathering support from wherever he can. The Engineers Order and the Duke of Herdforthbridge included."

"He's what?" Carmina laughed. "No, if Herdforthbridge supports him, Leythfordham must be his puppet. He's too dumb to come with such plans himself."

"Also, a few days ago, my friend's school in the same neighbourhood collapsed without reason. That is a bit too much of a coincidence."

"If you are talking about your master's daughter, I assure you nobody in your blasted society is fond of her charity."

She paused for a moment to pull the red velvet curtains and let the grey light of the day fill the room.

"Those bloody aristocrats spend their nights in establishments such as mine. Yet they despise their peers who stoop as low as to mingle openly with the destitute. They think London's poor are a liability for our almighty prosperous city, so it would be more profitable to get rid of them. The Marquess or whoever else is behind this won't stop until they silence Lady Hollingsworth."

"There is more." Jasper told her about the development during Edmund's dinner.

"So," he said, his eyes locked on her, "Carmina Harcourt, do you accept becoming my partner and informant again? We shall work as a team, as we used to before –"

"I do. But I am only doing this because I want to help those people and see the likes of Herdforthbridge squirm in misery. I have my own matters to settle with him."

OUT IN THE STREET, Jasper let out a sigh of relief, content to have secured Carmina's help. He had come to the Cinnamon Dove without much hope, but she proved to have more common sense than he had thought.

The harder part was to tell Edmund.

It wasn't even noon yet, and he expected Ivy Blackwell at the workshop in the afternoon. He had plenty of time to visit his brother.

At the skystation, while waiting for the gondotram, he tried – and failed – to imagine the best way to let him know about his teaming up with Carmina again. Still, as distressed as he was, Jasper couldn't hide a satisfied grin seeing Edmund's startled look when he entered his office at the Inspectorates.

"I expect something of the magnitude of a big earthquake to make you come here without being summoned with at least three notes and six speakerbox calls," the earl said. "Especially since you have an important meeting planned."

"I just had another important meeting I must inform you about. I asked Carmina to work with me again, and she agreed."

There, he said it. Now he waited for the imminent tempest to occur.

Edmund's face got one shade darker.

"No!" His brother's voice had the intensity of thunder. "Leave her out of this. I had my reasons to take her off that mission three years ago."

"You agreed to let me choose my team. She set her private matters aside, and I wish you do the same. This is not about whose pride is bigger. As I recall, she used to be your best agent."

"Bloody hell, Jasper!" Edmund shouted in an unexpected burst of anger. "You don't understand! Pride be damned, it is not about that! This mission might be too dangerous for someone as reckless as her! Do not drag her into this!"

"Try to trust her more. Carmina is still angry, and she doesn't want to see you again – but surely you know that. Don't offer a kind of protection she doesn't need! She didn't wish to leave Her Majesty's service. When it comes to her, you are a hypocrite. You *still* consider her your best agent, isn't that so?"

Edmund slumped back into his chair, propping his forehead in his hands.

"Yes, I do. And I *did not* release her from service," he said, without looking at Jasper, who was not used to seeing his brother in such a state. "I let her believe I did, but I never signed the papers. I couldn't. I always knew a day like this would come."

"Let her be," Jasper said. "If there is one person in London who can really help us, it's her. She's strong and doesn't need us to cripple or belittle her abilities in the name of safety. I shall work with her with or without your approval."

"All right," Edmund conceded, returning to his usual unreadable self. "I agree. As long as you design Her Majesty's airship and discover the truth about *The Golden Griffin* without fail, and with everyone alive."

~

WITH JASPER GONE, Edmund could collect his thoughts at last. He went to the windows, looking absently at the oversized cogwheel that rolled the artificial waterfall in the institution gardens. His eyes were staring at the tumbling stream of water, but his mind was back to the night he had last seen Carmina Harcourt, over three years before.

He still remembered vividly each detail of that evening. Her violet curls spread over her shoulders; the texture of her chemise; the stains and buckles on her leather corset and overskirt; her bare feet on the thick red carpet of her private study; the intoxicating taste of her lips when she stood on her tiptoes to welcome him with a kiss; the lavender fragrance of her neck. His memory still recalled how beautiful she was in the copper light of the lamps and how he hated himself for what he was about to do.

"I read your report." He let her off his arms and started pacing around the room, unable to stay still. "While I find it hard to believe the Duke of Herdforthbridge would get himself involved in a conspiracy, I shall not exclude this possibility. However, if your findings prove true, this investigation is more dangerous than we thought. He has not only immense power but also a good share of underground resources."

"This is why I am asking you to team me up with Jasper. We can solve this case together."

"I cannot do that. His full attention must be on *The Golden Griffin*. I must keep him away for a while, at least until we launch the royal airship and he receives the credit he deserves."

"All right, I shall do it alone. I must find out what that traitor of Herdforthbridge is concocting behind our backs. It ought to have something to do with *The Golden Griffin*. Otherwise, why would he say that the royal airship must not fly? I heard him talking to the Marquess of Leythfordham at Claridge's. He was pleading with him to make sure his request reached the Engineers Order, or else he would find other ways."

"Which doesn't make him the mastermind of a devilish plan against the Royal House. As much as he despises the Order, he would never harm Her Majesty."

"I do not trust him! If his intentions were good, he would have come to *you*! You would vouch for him no matter what, but I am almost certain he is scheming something. I shall find out what."

"And how exactly are you planning to find out?"

"By infiltrating into his mansion, of course," Carmina said matter-of-factly. "I am your best agent when it comes to disguise. I shall not fail."

"Letting you into his house alone is out of the question. We are talking about Oscar here! He would recognise you in an instant, regardless of your skill. There is another way, which brings me to the other purpose of my visit here tonight. As of now, I release you from service."

Carmina stopped where she stood, staring at him with bewildered eyes.

"Edmund, this kind of joke doesn't suit you. Release me from service? Just when I am about to uncover that bastard?"

"I told you there is another way. Which doesn't involve putting you in danger."

"Such as?"

"Such as I marrying his sister."

A heavy silence drifted in the room, as the enormity of what his words meant for both of them was sinking in. For a moment, he saw in her green eyes the same agonising pain he felt.

"I never thought I meant so little to you," Carmina said, her voice bitter and cold. "You don't love me enough to trust me. You would rather release me from service and leave me than letting me handle this case until the end. Whatever that end might be, it would have been more honourable for me than being disgraced in such a manner! Do this and I shall never forgive you!"

"Leave you? I do not recall saying anything about leaving you. I only said I shall marry Oscar's sister. I am pursuing this arranged marriage only because the importance of this matter requires so. This changes nothing between us."

"This changes *everything* between us! You couldn't have possibly imagined we would still be together if you married someone else. Such an idea is even more preposterous coming from someone as upright as you. Edmund, I am the woman you love, not your bloody whore! If you marry Herdforthbridge's sister, I shall ask you to stay away from me."

Another moment of silence filled Carmina's study. She

was angry and hurt, and it was his fault. He had been selfish to think he could follow his plan without losing her.

Insulting her dignity was the worst thing he could have done.

"You are right," he said. "So be it, I shall do as you say. If we are dealing with a case of sedition and Oscar discovers you investigating it, you could die. I am fine with you hating me as long as you are alive."

"Edmund, just leave and spare me of your pathetic protection, which I have never asked for. I wish you trusted me more instead of deciding that a life as dull as a rock, confined in this bloody establishment is what I need."

"Carmina, this is far from what I want. But it might be the best option we have. If Oscar is indeed plotting something and *The Golden Griffin* is in danger, he will kill you without blinking. However, if I marry Emmeline Rexworth, she will lead me straight to him. She is connected not only with every noble house in England, but with the Engineers Order as well. Nobody will suspect anything, since my mother has always wanted this marriage."

"Then, at least one person will be happy." Carmina was gazing at the maps on her wall, her voice stern and distant. "It never bothered me that nobody but Herdforthbridge knew about us, because we loved each other so much and I needed nothing else. Now, we must give up everything for the sake of duty. Our hearts, our dreams, our plans to travel and see the world. Edmund, do as you wish. But I only hope our paths will never cross again."

Three years later, fate mocked them enough to make them cross paths.

~

"Miss Ivy, are you certain you want to do this?" Mrs Carraway whined at the young woman who was opening the door to leave the house. Outside, Edmund Asher's driver was waiting for her in the steammotor. "We can still live decently, even if you only keep your contract with Lady Hollingsworth. Don't give away your parents' work! Not after you tried so hard to hide and protect it!"

"I am not *giving away* anything, Eudora," Ivy said, trying not to lose her temper. "I will work on it myself while *being paid* for it! Besides, aren't you always saying how much you trust that lordship of yours? Time has come to test that trust myself."

She closed the door without waiting for her nursemaid's answer. As much as she loved Mrs Carraway, sometimes it was better to slip away until the storm passed.

It was indeed unusual that the Earl of Wyverstone was also her maid's employer, but she preferred to consider it only a harmless coincidence. She needed to trust his intentions.

The steammotor stopped at the address the earl had indicated at their first meeting. Ivy got off and pressed the small copper button next to the workshop entrance.

Her heart was beating fast, while she tried to imagine her first encounter with Jasper Kendall Asher. She had heard so much about him from her parents, and from the articles she used to read in the Engineers Order's journal. A brilliant mind, and one of the best airship engineers in England. And she would work with him. Her Mama and Papa would have been proud of her.

The door opened, revealing the earl's brother. She gaped, in a failed attempt to match the man in front of her with the image in her mind. Though he had Edmund Asher's handsome features and blue eyes, he was not as tall and commanding as him. His sleeves were rolled up to his elbows, his shirt and brown trousers kept visible traces of oil and grease, and his dishevelled raven locks desperately needed a comb. He looked more human and less intimidating than in her imagination.

"How do you do, Miss Blackwell," he said with a polite, yet distant smile. "I am Jasper Kendall Asher, but please call me Jasper. Since we shall work together, it is only natural to call each other by our names, from one engineer to another."

I am not quite an engineer, Ivy thought, extending her hand to shake his. She liked him and his workshop. Regardless of her nursemaid's complaints that he never allowed her to touch anything in that room, it looked neat. Everything was stored orderly on long tables and in high cabinets. Airship scale models sat on wooden shelves, and the only objects on his desk were the speakerbox and some papers. His workbench was empty and clean.

"The Earl of Wyverstone told me we would work on Her Majesty's airship." Ivy sipped from the cup of tea Jasper had poured for her, inhaling its delicate jasmine fragrance. "The only reason I agreed was to see my parents' work completed and acknowledged. I can't forget *The Golden Griffin* and how they died, so don't expect me to be grateful for this opportunity."

"No, I have no right to ask for such a thing. Whatever you think of Her Majesty is not my concern," he said in a rather cold and dismissive tone. "I only want us to create the most amazing airship ever made, with Octavia and Chalford's help. I shall think of that as the only reason you'll come to my workshop."

"Then I'm leaving this here." Ivy placed on his desk the cylindrical leather case she carried on her shoulder. "These are my parents' plans for the new airship they were planning to build. They left them with me when they last visited Paris, one week before they died. Otherwise, they would have been lost. Our home was plundered soon after *The Golden Griffin.*"

"I remember. The Engineers Order filed an investigation request, but the constabulary dismissed the incident as petty thievery."

"Rats and caterpillars, that was as petty thievery as I am the Queen of England!" Ivy's cheeks were red with anger. Her temper was getting hold of her again. "I had to return to France right after my parents' funeral, to settle things for my moving back to London. While I was gone, our house was turned upside down, yet nothing was missing. Nothing! Not a bloody coin! How is that petty thievery?"

Jasper rested his hand on the leather case that enclosed the Blackwells' drawings and notes.

"No, it was not petty thievery. The intruders were most probably after these. They were not mere thieves, but people who knew exactly what they wanted."

"Now, do you understand why I tried so hard to hide them? Why I wanted no one to know I had those papers? My parents made me live as another person, under another name, in another country, and I believe it was because of those documents. I don't know how your brother found out about them, but now I have no choice but to trust you. Jasper Kendall Asher, you must give me your word you won't betray my trust."

"Ivy Blackwell, I give you my word." Jasper extended his hand, his voice softer and kinder. "Your parents' airship plans are safe with me. I shall protect them as well as you did. You and I shall turn your parents' airship into reality, together. I promise you that."

Jasper's words offered her a strange sense of comfort and confidence. When she took his hand, her doubts faded. He saw her as his peer, regarded them as a team. His talk about the new airship as their shared project gave her the assurance she needed so much.

"Thank you." Ivy smiled at him with a new sense of relief. "Eudora was right. I believe I can trust you. Let's create the most amazing airship ever made."

~

IVY REACHED the airharbour and ran towards the suspended dock where she had berthed *The Skycradle*. She didn't want to be late on the first day of her contract, but her visit to the workshop was important enough for that compromise. To her dismay, Lady Hollingsworth had arrived, along with the Killen brothers and three other children.

"Oh, Miss Blackwell, please forgive me," Rowena Hollingsworth said. "We came earlier than planned because I wanted to show the children around the airharbour. I hope we are not much of a hindrance to you."

"Not at all," Ivy said, grateful for her employer's manners. "I don't need much time to prepare my ship. We'll be airborne soon enough."

A few minutes later, they were flying above London. Rowena's voice explaining about the history of their capital seemed miles away. Ivy was in her own little world, where only *The Skycradle* and her navigation board existed.

The awkward humming of the pressure gauges brought her back to reality. She checked the dials, unable to understand. The pre-flight checks had shown no issue. *The Skycradle*'s pipes and systems worked, so the gas should have been valved by then. Yet the pressure was increasing without a drop of it being released. If that went on, the gasbags would burst while they were over three hundred feet above the ground. She calculated the time she needed to land, setting the craft on its return course to the airharbour.

"We are going back!" she announced, keeping her eyes on the pressure dials.

"Is anything the matter? Are we safe?" As hard as she tried to keep her composure, Rowena was visibly distressed.

"The relief valves stopped working," Ivy said, glancing at starboard through her goggles. Fortunately, the berth was close. She would soon release the anchorage grapples.

"What does it mean? Will the ship explode? Will the children die?" Rowena's eyes were almost dark, and her hands were trembling.

Ivy frowned, baffled at her employer's exaggerated reaction.

"Lady Hollingsworth, no one will die. The gas in *The Skycradle*'s gasbags can't flow out. This means it's expanding until the bags will burst. I noticed this on time, and we are close to the airharbour. We'll make it. However, something is wrong. Hell knows why anyone would do this to me, but I think someone has bloody rigged my ship!"

7

The sun had almost set when Jasper stood up, with a wide grin on his face. After reading for the second time all the documents Ivy Blackwell had given him, plenty of ideas crossed his mind to complete the airship drafted by her parents.

He finally understood why those plans had to be hidden and protected so well, why the two engineers had been elusive with their research, and why Edmund's theory proved to be right.

Completing what they had begun would be not only an honour but also a challenge to his skills. He knew almost nothing about the daughter, but she ought to be familiar with airships. After all, she had graduated from the engineering school in Paris and owned a craft.

Jasper stared at his workbench, realising he had started to accept the happiness that was slowly making its way inside him. After such a long time of self-denial, he was ready to return. The following day he would start drawing his own prototype, the first in three years. A draft of what he intended to be the most astonishing airship ever built in England. It was a far-fetched ambition, but, after seeing the Blackwells' plans, it seemed possible.

Such a busy yet fulfilling day ought to end with a well-deserved glass of gin and a cheerful chat at the Copper Kettle. He hid Ivy's leather case and opened the door to go and put his idea into practice.

Only to bump into Rowena at his doorstep.

This might not be a fulfilling day, and I might not drink my gin, after all.

Rowena Hollingsworth would never visit him unchaperoned at such a late hour unless something was dreadfully wrong.

"Jasper, I need your help. Someone is after me, and innocent people might suffer because of that. I have proof, but I doubt the constable will listen."

For a split second, he heard Carmina's words in the back of his mind. *The Marquess or whoever else is behind this won't stop until they silence Lady Hollingsworth.*

Jasper let her in. "Did you find out something about your school? Or have a hint about who might be behind that demolition stunt?"

"No, even worse. I don't know who, or why, but they tried again. I was so scared! I thought I would see *The Golden Griffin* all over again!"

Jasper's face turned white.

"What did you say?" he asked, trying to keep his voice steady. "Rowena, where were you? And with whom?"

"I was having my classes in that airship. Today was my navigator's first day of contract, yet we had to return to the airharbour. Otherwise, the gasbags would have burst. Jasper, she said her ship was rigged! I am certain it has something to do with me!"

A cold sweat ran down his spine, while a sense of dread

was crawling into his chest. To his knowledge, female navigators were a rarity.

"*She*? *Who* is your navigator?"

"Ivy Blackwell. I don't want to involve her in my mess! I need to find out who is after me and why, before I put other innocent people in danger! She and the children could have died today on my account!"

Jasper took her hands in his.

"Rowena, where is she? Where is your navigator now?"

"At the airharbour, to check her airship's ducts and valves. I shouldn't have dragged her in this!"

"I'm leaving," he said, rushing to the door. Ivy was his charge. If anything happened to her, it would be his fault. He couldn't disappoint Edmund from the first day of his return. "I shall halt a carriage to take you home, but please forgive me. This time I cannot accompany you. I must go to the airharbour."

"To the airharbour? You?"

"Yes, I," he said, looking into Rowena's startled eyes. "I cannot avoid that place forever. I cannot explain now, but they aren't only after you. If that airship was indeed rigged, chances are they were after Ivy. She is Octavia and Chalford Blackwell's daughter."

"Oh, God! I should have realised that. Please, Jasper, whatever you are planning to do, be safe. Both of you, be safe."

Less than ten minutes later, Rowena was on her way to the Hollingsworth mansion, while Jasper ran like mad to the skystation.

~

Up in *The Skycradle*'s envelope, Ivy crawled along the isolated narrow space sandwiched between the cargo hold and the upper half that hid the gasbags, checking the valves and ducts of her airship.

Dirty and tired, she dreamt of a good rest and something to eat. But her anger was stronger than her wish for comfort. The way Hadrian Hayes – chief clerk of the Airharbour Assignments Office – had dismissed her was outrageous and unacceptable. And hard to forget.

"Miss Blackwell, please understand. Nobody went to your docking berth! Not this morning, not this afternoon, not ever," he'd said, exasperated. "Have you gone mad? Why would anyone rig an old airship such as yours?"

"This is what I am trying to find out. I need you to tell me who the bloody hell was up there on my berth today. *The Skycradle* would not go nuts without reason! I know my craft!"

"Look here, Miss Blackwell. I am tired of your fits and stunts. You seem to forget that the only reason you are here is because of your late parents – God bless their souls. But I will not tolerate such behaviour any longer. Stop blaming others for your incompetence!"

Ivy had left slamming the door, knowing that it was useless to insist. The old man could never stand her. She shouldn't have expected anything in the first place. Yet, the way he treated her made her feel insignificant. If she were a weakling, she would have cried. But a woman who had to fend for herself all alone couldn't afford tears.

"Rats and caterpillars!" Ivy swore loudly, her echo resonating in the small enclosure where she was lying on her back. "I hope your damned bones will feed the maggots in the deepest pit of hell, you old filthy bastard!"

She hardly finished her heartfelt cursing when she heard someone climbing up the ladder that connected the gondola to the envelope. She froze, one thousand possibilities going through her mind in less than a second.

"Ivy! Ivy Blackwell, are you up there?" A man's voice shouted from the cargo hold. She vaguely remembered that voice – deep and slightly hoarse – and it took her only a few moments to put a face to it.

"Yes, I'm here! Use the ladder in the back!"

But Jasper Asher was already in front of her.

"Someone must have really upset you, for you to swear in such manner," he said. "I wouldn't want to be in their shoes."

"Why are you here?" Ivy asked, annoyed and in no mood to play the host. "If this is about Her Majesty's airship, I hope it can wait until tomorrow. I have some other matters to take care of at the moment."

Jasper kneeled underneath a duct next to her, ignoring her surly reception. "Your employer happens to be my close friend. She told me you might use some help. What makes you think your ship was rigged?"

"It looks like someone blocked the relief valves," she said, more gently. "They had no problem. However, during my last flight, they failed to release the gas. I must find out what clogged them, but I can't detect anything faulty with the vents."

"I think you are looking in the wrong place." Jasper squinted above. "It's not the valves, but what prevents the gas from getting to them."

Half crouched, he disengaged the narrow duct which connected the first gasbag to the external valve, revealing the lid. As Ivy expected, it was open.

"What the bloody hell happened? If the flap was open, why is all the gas still in there?"

Jasper showed her the tubular edge of the pipe, obstructed by a rigid white cluster. "Because of this. The insulation clogged the duct. I expect the same for the rest of them. Why did you choose such material?"

"I didn't! I asked the airharbour mechanics to examine *The Skycradle* for my new contract. But she passed all my pre-flight checks. If something were wrong, I would have seen in the pressure gauges! Someone messed with the valves!"

"This kind of foam expands and goes solid at the contact with the gas," Jasper said, matter-of-factly. "It was a technical error. They insulated the gasbag flaps with too much material, which blocked the ducts. *The Skycradle* wasn't rigged."

She stared at him as if to find a hidden meaning in his words. But his eyes seemed honest enough to offer her the reassurance she needed.

He smiled, offering his hand. "Ivy, no one is after you. The blockage was an error, and I shall help you mend it. Let's fix the rest of the ducts so that *The Skycradle* can fly again."

Ivy took his hand and sat up. She was beginning to trust Jasper. He cared enough to come all the way from the workshop to the airharbour to help her, although they barely knew each other. It was all that mattered to her. Though she doubted she could have discovered the insulation problem by herself, at least now she understood what had happened. Perhaps she should go back and apologise to Mr Hayes.

But her forgiving abilities did not extend that far.

"HOLD IT STEADY," Jasper said, tightening the gripping cap over the pipe and the upper vent. "Done!" he added a few moments later, after attaching the last duct to the flap of the last gasbag, with Ivy's help.

Both of them were grinning happily, covered in white

dust, their hands smeared up to their elbows. The sun had long set when they finished cleaning up all the pipes which connected the vents of the gasbags to the external relief valves.

"Shall we lift this beauty up into the sky to check how she fares?" Ivy asked. "I reckon I've never seen London's night sky from up there."

Jasper's grin faded. He had avoided airships since Jade's death. In his rush to the airharbour, it never crossed his mind that he could end up flying again.

Yet he couldn't let Ivy sense his distress. Not after he had summoned his full ability of dissimulation to convince her it was a technical error.

He didn't want to scare her. However, he was certain that, whoever it was who inspected *The Skycradle*, they blocked the ducts on purpose. He had to convince Ivy everything was fine. Even if that meant fighting his own fears.

They climbed down into the gondola, and Ivy uncovered the viewing deck. She stopped next to her pilot seat in front of the board.

"Is anything the matter?" Jasper asked, coming beside her. "Worry not. She should be as good as new now."

"It's not that," she said, without looking at him, staring into the distance. "I never let anyone pilot *The Skycradle*, but I always wanted to see the sky from my viewing deck as a passenger. To experience what my customers must feel."

She turned to him with pleading eyes. "Jasper, I know that among the first things an airship engineer learns in England is how to fly a craft. I doubt you are an exception to the rule, so may I ask you to pilot her? Only this time?"

He froze. In his mind, fragments of memories were struggling to break the barrier he had so carefully built to keep himself sane. The blazing flames engulfing *The Golden*

Griffin; the burnt carcass of the airship fallen on the barren land of the airharbour; the unrecognisable body of his twin brother.

A cold sweat covered his shaky hands. He hated that place. He hated it as much as he loved it.

Jasper wiped his hands on his trousers, trying to steady his breath. He hadn't touched a navigation board for three years. He had kept away from the airharbour for three years. Each time he craved to return there, among crafts and engines, he refrained.

Everything out of fear to relive that night.

Until the blasted moment when he needed to make sure Ivy was safe. Half of him wanted to flee without looking back. But he couldn't run like a coward and leave her. The other half admitted that Master Hollingsworth was right. He missed flying, so Ivy's offer could be an opportunity for him to kill his demons and return to the sky he loved so much.

He led her to the open deck, his hand on her shoulder. "All right. The night sky is yours. Leave the flying to me."

Jasper returned to the board, sat down, and put on the navigator goggles, taking a deep breath. He remembered all the commands and buttons as if he had never taken such a long break.

With a steady hand, he turned on the engines, checked the lifting gas and pressure gauges, and released the anchorage grapples, getting *The Skycradle* airborne with the precision of a compass.

It was an unusually clear sky, with plenty of stars and a crescent moon. The air was crisp and chilly, and a faint stale smell of earth, metal and coal made its way from the airharbour through the open space at starboard.

"Beautiful!" Ivy said, with an intoxicating laugh, her elbows propped on the railing. "So bloody beautiful!"

"Oh, yes!" Jasper agreed, taking in the magnificent view of the night sky. "Airships are so bloody beautiful!"

After three years he was free, and the feeling was exhilarating.

~

"I'll walk you home." Jasper looked with a guilty frown at his pocket watch that showed a bit before midnight. Had he not accepted her request to fly *The Skycradle*, Ivy would have been safely back by then. "I cannot leave you alone at such an hour. Mrs Carraway must be dead worried."

"She will recover when she sees me," Ivy said, her voice betraying the same amount of guilt. "First, she will be busy lecturing me for an hour about the proper conduct of an educated young woman. After that, with some luck, I might be allowed to go to sleep. If I want the latter to happen sooner, I should go home now."

Jasper laughed, offering his arm. Luckily, the carriage they halted on their way considerably reduced the time it took them to get to Ivy's house in Clerkenwell.

"Thank you." Ivy's voice was almost a whisper in the mild darkness of the vehicle. "It's unusual for me to receive help like this. I never ask for it, and I never receive it. It's just how it is."

"I have the talent to be in the right place at the right moment for ladies who are not accustomed to asking for help," he said with a grin. "My day started with fixing a boiler and ended with fixing an airship."

"I never ask for help because I have no one to turn to," she replied. "After my parents died, I only had Eudora and my airship. All those important people who used to call on Mama and Papa vanished after *The Golden Griffin*. When I moved back to London, nobody ever asked how the Blackwells' daughter was faring. Who would care about a pathetic orphan? This is why what you did today is important to me."

Jasper didn't answer. Her words pierced through his heart, reaching the darkest corners of his being. He thought of himself, of his first year after Jade's death. He had Edmund, Rowena, his master, and the people at the Copper Kettle offering him all the support he needed, while he kept rejecting them. The young woman in front of him had lost almost everything, with no one left around. For the first time in his life, he felt self-centred and ashamed.

8

"You are saying someone might be after her." Edmund inhaled the rich aroma of his brandy before taking a sip. "Perhaps someone found out she has the Blackwells' last airship plans. Though it makes little sense to want her killed."

"I fail to find *any* sense in *anything* that keeps happening lately," Jasper said. He liked talking to his brother in the dead of night in his study, without anyone in the Wyverstone mansion knowing he was there. It was like in the old times when he and Edmund worked as a team, and Jade was still alive. "Rowena lost her school. Shortly after, someone tried to rig Ivy's airship. These incidents might be connected. It's my gut feeling."

"You forget one crucial thing," Edmund said with the sharpness of a blade, his blue eyes as cold as the night sky. "We are not working based on gut feelings, but on evidence. It is your duty to find it, as is mine to support you in this endeavour. An excellent opportunity will be Leythfordham's banquet on his father's birthday. I secured an invitation for you as well. It grants you full access into his house. You only need to find the right moment to look here and there without attracting too much attention."

"I figured as much," Jasper said. "Speaking of which, I need your help. They will need more staff for the ball. Carmina wants to send Hazel to sniff around during these two weeks of preparations. She will smooth the way for me and keep a close watch on the marquess. But they won't hire the first girl in need of a job who shows up on their doorstep. She needs a reference letter from a respectable family."

"Of course." Edmund opened one of his desk's drawers, producing a note written in exquisite calligraphy on creamy thick paper. "I cannot think of someone more respectable than the dowager Countess of Wyverstone to recommend poor *Amelia Hartling* as a maid for the Duchess of Litchborough's household. Hardworking as she is, they will want to keep her for good."

Jasper recognised the unmistakable penmanship of their mother – dowager Countess of Wyverstone and an old friend of the Marquess of Leythfordham's mother.

"How did you even know to ask for this letter? Did Carmina forgive you and reach out to you? She came up with the idea only this afternoon, yet you've already prepared what we need."

"Alas, no." Edmund lifted one corner of his mouth in a grimace – one of the rare moments his usually unfathomable face had an expression. "I don't think she ever will after what I've done. Carmina's mind and mine are so much alike, so I knew what to do. I sent word to Mother right after you told me you are working with her again."

"Thank you." Jasper hid the paper in his pocket. "Now, a more urgent matter is Ivy. She might be in danger. If anyone else has heard of those papers' content, they would want her out of their way to find them.

"I cannot be sure whether her parents gave the slightest hint to the Inspectorates or at least to the Engineers Order. Their work concerned not only a new airship but also an innovation which could dramatically change airship engineering." He saw Edmund's eyes sparkling with interest. "Octavia and Chalford Blackwell were one step away from patenting the use of a new lifting gas."

Edmund stared at the intricate pattern of the iron frames which encased the tall windows, pondering the new bit of information.

"This detail changes everything we had for this case, so we must find out who else knew about it." He finally spoke, pouring another glass of brandy. "I told you I visited them once in Glenbuck, but they never said anything about their work. That explains their unexpected trip to Paris right before testing *The Golden Griffin*. Someone must have caught wind of their invention and wanted it. That explains the plundering of their house as well. And I'm afraid that –"

He stopped, and they shared a raw look of realisation.

"– they might be the very reason for what happened to *The Golden Griffin*." Jasper finished his brother's sentence with a strangled voice. "Someone has found out about their discovery and wants Ivy. We need to move her to a safer place, and the safest I can think of is the Hollingsworth mansion. She is Rowena's navigator, which means nobody will ask questions. But we must convince her."

"An excellent idea. I shall make sure Lady Hollingsworth extends the offer, and that Miss Blackwell won't reject it."

"How?"

"Leave that to me." Edmund put the brandy decanter back into the cabinet, indicating that their nocturnal meeting was over.

Outside, the darkness was slowly receding before the

hazy light heralding the dawn against a cloudy sky. It was the perfect time to stop by at the Cinnamon Dove and give Carmina the letter. That detour would take his mind off the new possibilities which connected the Blackwells to the core of *The Golden Griffin* incident.

Jasper had always thought it had been a warning for the Royal House – and for him, who had been in charge of the airship's engines. However, Jade might have been only a collateral victim caught in a whirlwind of events which had nothing to do with either of them.

The idea made him shiver, and he instinctively hugged himself. The streets were still deserted. High above, the silent gondotram tracks were looming like huge iron seams, in the wind that felt as cold and empty as his soul.

~

JASPER SQUINTED AT MRS CARRAWAY, visibly trying to suppress a yawn. "I would love a big jug of coffee this morning. Please prepare some tea for Ivy, and scones for all of us."

"Scones!? You are a nobleman, yet you call that breakfast?" Ivy protested. "I'm hungry. I'm expecting at least some ham, eggs, cheese, perhaps pudding as well? Eudora makes the best pudding –"

"God forbid, Miss Ivy!" Mrs Carraway lamented in horror. "For once, can you *behave*? An educated young woman never asks a gentleman for food! My lord, please forgive her. She means no harm. This savage just lacks proper manners."

"No, I should be the one apologising for being so inconsiderate. Prepare a decent breakfast with everything she asked for. I wouldn't want my partner to die of starvation in my house before we could even start working."

Jasper smiled, a clear sign that he was amused rather than irritated. If he was Rowena Hollingsworth's close friend and the brother of an earl, he must be accustomed to ladies who knew how to behave. Who didn't curse or demand breakfast in the house of a man whom they only met twice. Who didn't wear an old aeronaut outfit as their everyday clothes.

Ivy's cheeks were burning, the events of the previous day still vivid in her mind. She was too self-conscious around him, a discovery that didn't make her happy. The tiny red strands in his eyes marking the lack of sleep; his black hair tousled over his ears, the oil stain on the left sleeve of his shirt; his long, slender fingers when he extended his hand to greet her. She was keenly aware of all those insignificant details she wouldn't usually bother herself with.

That made her angry and ashamed.

He sat at his working bench, while Mrs Carraway disappeared into the small kitchen of the workshop to prepare breakfast. Ivy helped him spread her parents' drafts and plans on the wooden board.

"I read everything." Jasper stared at the small letters and figures of her father's handwriting. "If we could use your parents' discovery, it would mean a new era for airships. But first, I need your help to understand something."

"I expected you would." Ivy flipped through the papers and took out one filled with formulae and sketches of airship envelopes. "I believe you want more information about the new lifting gas Mama and Papa wrote about, for that is the core of the entire concept."

"Exactly. According to their findings, this gas has no colour and no smell, and is lighter than any other gas. The only problem is that we need to make sure we can produce it. It doesn't even have a name."

"As you know, they worked in Scotland for a while." Ivy

started pacing around the room, too nervous to remain seated. She had never talked to anyone about her parents' research before. "They obtained it after a year of relentless work, countless days spent in the Glenbuck colliery, and countless experiments with countless chemical reactions. A gas lighter than air, without the flammable hurdle of hydrogen. They extracted it from natural gas after separating it from methane. The entire formula is there, in those papers. But they died before naming or presenting their discovery to the world."

Ivy swallowed the stingy bitterness of her words. The most important work of her parents, *their most astonishing discovery*, was a nameless pile of papers filled with explanations and formulae. She wondered whether they could really turn them into the airship Octavia and Chalford Blackwell had envisioned. For the first time since she agreed to the Earl of Wyverstone's proposal, she doubted her choice.

"A lifting gas that would replace hydrogen and allow features we have only dreamt of until now. If we replicate your parents' experiments and prove them valid at an affordable cost, we could devise a heating system for airships without fearing they would blast. We could use generators and electric light! It would be indeed a marvel of an airship!" Jasper started sketching, only to stop a few moments later, his eyes fixed on Ivy with a worried frown.

"Did they tell anyone about their research in Scotland? Who else knows about this?"

"The Senior Lord of the Engineers Order, Benedict Quimby," Ivy said promptly. "Mama and Papa needed sponsorship from the Order for their research, so they had to tell him. He provided the money and visited them from time to time, to check the progress of their work. This is all I know. After their discovery, my parents rushed to Paris to leave all their drafts with me. They told me to protect those papers at all costs. One week later –"

"It's all right." Jasper interrupted her abruptly, as if he were eager to change the course of their conversation. "We'll retake Octavia and Chalford's experiment. If we succeed, we'll create the most amazing airship ever seen."

"We must think of a name," Ivy said. "For the lifting gas."

Jasper went to the big drawing board on the red brick wall and gazed at it for one long moment.

"Lighter than any other gas," he mumbled as he wrote, while Ivy watched curiously next to him.

"L-A-E-V-I-U-M," she spelt, loud and clear, trying to make sense of the big fat letters he was scribbling. "*Laevium*. Isn't that Latin? What was the word for lightweight? Laevis?"

"Precisely." Jasper turned to her with a satisfied grin. "What do you say?"

"I declare you the godparent of this new lifting gas. But we need to replicate Mama and Papa's experiments and reach the same result. How are we going to do that? Their laboratory is in Glenbuck."

His face brightened up in a wide smile, just as Mrs Carraway entered the working room with the breakfast tray.

"But of course, we're going to Scotland!"

ROWENA STOPPED in front of the private library where her father had received Edmund Asher. The Earl of Wyverstone's visit at almost six in the afternoon was unexpected, though not as unusual as her presence at their meeting. Something must have happened, but she couldn't fathom what. She only hoped Jasper wasn't in trouble. Last time she'd seen him, he was running to the airharbour, and she hadn't heard from him since.

She mustered her courage to enter the room.

The two men were drinking brandy in a quite relaxed atmosphere. Which meant no impending catastrophe was looming.

Edmund stood to greet her. "Good afternoon, Lady Hollingsworth. I apologise for coming at such an unsuitable hour, but I believe that what I am going to tell you will bring you enough joy to forgive my rudeness."

"You are always welcome in our house, my lord," Rowena said with a curtsey. "All the more when you bring cheerful news. We need it after the unfortunate recent events."

He handed her a document.

"As of today, you can resume your highly regarded activities in St. Giles. Moreover, you will receive a new place for them, close to your old school. The property belonged to the Duke of Herdforthbridge, but he accepted my suggestion to donate it. I do hope the building suits your taste. It used to be a warehouse, but we shall refurbish it to fit its new purpose."

Rowena read the paper in astonishment. The place was large enough to fit a proper school, without being always forced to improvise and mingle children with grown-ups to accommodate everyone.

"In usual circumstances, I would accept your kind offer, for which I am grateful." She put the document on the mahogany desk, before turning to Edmund. "However, I already have a contract for my new school, which I cannot nullify. It would be too disrespectful towards Miss Blackwell."

"My child, this is an opportunity you cannot miss," Theophilus Hollingsworth said. "You can still keep your other contract. Use it to take your pupils from time to time for a flight over London. They would enjoy such trips more without being obliged to pay attention to their lessons."

"Miss Blackwell has another assignment," Edmund said. "She will work with Jasper to design Her Majesty's airship. It won't be that troublesome if she stops using *The Skycradle* as a flying school."

Rowena could not hide her amazement, finally understanding how Jasper knew her navigator. Ivy was chosen for such an important project. Jasper accepted her, and even faced one of his worst fears, running to the airharbour to make sure she was all right. Perhaps her contract hadn't been worthy enough of Miss Blackwell. She might actually do her a favour if she invalidated it.

"Thank you for your kindness," Rowena said. "Since I must inform Miss Blackwell myself, I shall kindly ask you to excuse me. I need to call on her."

JASPER STARED in disbelief at the devastation they found in Ivy's house. The few pieces of furniture were scattered upside down. All the drawers of the massive wooden desk were out. Papers and other stationery were thrown on the floor. Even Mrs Carraway's sewing basket had its content discarded on the carpet.

He had accompanied Ivy and her nursemaid home, in a rare attempt to behave like a proper gentleman. Only to be welcomed by the desolate image of a ransacked place. Not one thing was in its rightful spot. The rooms seemed to have witnessed the fury of a thunderstorm.

"What in the devil's name happened here?" he said, not sure how to react to such an unexpected sight. "How can someone plunder a house in broad daylight? I thought there was a limit even for a neighbourhood of miscreants such as Clerkenwell."

"Rats and caterpillars, what plunder!" Ivy planted her fist into the wall of the drawing room. "I've seen this before! Nothing is missing. They came with a purpose! But what they are looking for is no longer here!"

"Do you think they are after your parents' plans again?" Jasper asked. "Perhaps they found out you had them?"

"Then you might be in danger! Miss Blackwell, you cannot stay here with the house turned into a battlefield, chased by hoodlums paid by Lord knows who!"

Rowena's voice made everyone turn to her.

Only then Jasper realised he hadn't even called her on the speakerbox to let her know he was all right after his rush to the airharbour. During his nocturnal escapade in *The Skycradle*, he felt the closest to happy he had been in the last three years. So much so that it made him oblivious of how worried Rowena must have been on his account. Jasper rested one hand on her shoulder, his blue eyes sending unspoken apologies.

He sensed something was wrong, for she would never come to someone's house without announcing herself first. It was his turn to worry.

"Rowena, is anything the matter? It is not like you to call on people like this at such hours."

"Your brother came today with a proposal for my school, and I needed to speak to Miss Blackwell about an important matter. But it is neither the time nor the place for that. Miss Blackwell, I apologise for barging in like this, but the door was open. Please accept my invitation to be my guest for a while. Along with Mrs Carraway, of course. At least until we discover who did this and why."

For Jasper, all the pieces clicked into place. *I shall make sure Lady Hollingsworth extends the offer, and that Miss Blackwell won't reject it*, his brother had said. And, in less than a day, Rowena was indeed extending her courtesy to Ivy in the most natural way possible.

Edmund had put the perfect plan into action. Though, by Jasper's books, he had gone way too far.

A stark reminder of what a terrible force Edmund Asher was. The earl could make anyone his puppet, just by pulling the right strings. But, as much as he disagreed with his brother's plan, he ought to help him.

"You should accept," he said, turning to Ivy again. "Besides, you will love the Hollingsworth house. They have a most excellent cook, so you will have the benefit of a royal breakfast each morning."

"That would be a good reason to consider," Ivy said in a shaky voice, gazing at an old painting on the wall. "Thank you, Lady Hollingsworth. I accept your kindness. I assure you it won't be for long."

"You can stay at our house for as long as you need. We are most happy to receive you as our guest."

WITH IVY safely settled in Rowena's house, Jasper hurried to the Inspectorates. With a bit of luck, he would find Benedict Quimby still there.

He entered the office just when the Senior Lord was leaving.

"I apologise for coming this late. I need some answers about something important, and you are the only one who could provide them."

"Of course." Quimby took his gold tipped cane and started towards the door, with a smile on his round plump face. "But I suggest we talk outside. It would be a pity to miss this delightful sunset."

Jasper followed him on the walking lane surrounding the mechanical waterfall, which seemed even bigger from up close. The water kept plunging from the gigantic iron cogwheel into the pool at its base, a blue and copper drop against the sky that still held the last traces of the sun. The round metallic clock on top of it showed eight. Enough time before he went to the airharbour.

"So, what is this important thing you want to talk about?" Quimby asked, tugging his bowler over the thick white wisps of his hair.

"Who else knew of Octavia and Chalford Blackwell's discovery? Did you tell anyone about their new lifting gas?"

The Senior Lord of the Engineers Order stopped, eyeing Jasper with a doubtful look.

"How do *you* know about that? They told me they informed no one but me about their research. Are the Classified Affairs investigating this? Is it your brother's doing?"

"No," Jasper said, surprised at Quimby's reaction. "Edmund has nothing to do with this. I heard about that gas from their daughter. Ivy is working with me. She told me about her parents' research, how those papers burnt with *The Golden Griffin.* A pity indeed. But now someone is after her. They might have erroneously believed she had those documents and have tried to rig her ship. I need to know if you've told anyone else about the Blackwells' work in Scotland."

Quimby made a dismissive gesture with his cane. "That research was mere fantasy. Those two had a brilliant idea, but they never reached any result. Obviously, I told no one – since

I had nothing to tell about. A lot of wasted energy – and money, if you ask me."

"You mean they never completed their research? Are you sure?"

"Absolutely. You should focus on more important things. Jasper, you are an airship engineer, not a detective. If Miss Blackwell feels threatened, she should inform the constabulary." He glanced at the waterfall clock. The daylight had already faded. "Now, if you'll excuse me, my carriage is waiting. I have refitted my mech-horses with new steel cables and eye-lights, and I cannot wait to check the improvement."

Benedict Quimby had returned to his usual good-natured demeanour, yet something about him made Jasper apprehensive. But he understood. The man couldn't just blabber about such a secret matter to anyone who came and asked. It was in the Order's best interest if he kept his mouth shut.

QUIMBY'S CARRIAGE disappeared from Jasper's sight, leaving him with more doubts instead of clearing them. But he would not leave the Inspectorates empty-handed. If the Senior Lord had no answers for him, he would find them in the Engineers Order's Archives.

The Archives were off limits to regular members – of course, a detail far too insignificant to stop him.

"Are you not supposed to be at the airharbour?" Edmund asked, squinting at him when he entered his office. "It's almost night."

"Later. Now I need to search for something in the Engineers Order's Archives. Will you let me use your secret passage to the basement?"

"If you are caught, you are on your own. Remember that."

Edmund opened a cabinet and retrieved a piece of paper. He copied the content and gave it to his brother, before putting the original back. Jasper stared at the weird combination of letters, figures, and strange symbols.

"The cypher of the Engineers Order's Archives entrance," Edmund explained. "This will spare you the time to unlock it. I suppose you were not expecting an open door waiting for you."

"How did you convince Quimby to share it? Only a select few have access to the Archives. He would swallow that cypher rather than giving it willingly."

"He doesn't know I have it. Master Hollingsworth figured it out for me to have access if need be. I never trusted the Engineers Order."

"You are starting to sound like Herdforthbridge," Jasper said, hiding the code in his pocket, while Edmund pushed a bookshelf, revealing the floor.

He shifted the brass sconce on the wall, and a small square in the wooden parquet slid underneath. Jasper crouched, ready to climb two floors down the iron ladder.

"I shall wait for you here. No one will suspect anything if they see us leaving the Inspectorates together. And be careful, mind you."

Jasper nodded and descended into the basement. As soon as he reached the ground, the piece of floor above moved back, leaving him in darkness.

Feeling his way ahead, he followed the narrow corridor until he reached a dead end and stopped near the wall to listen.

Nothing but overwhelming silence.

He pushed aside one large stone slab at the base and crawled into the aisle where several doors marked the entrances to the Orders' Archives. In the dim light of the bulbs mounted into the walls, the main passageway was stretching empty and silent beyond the locked iron grate.

Inside the Engineers Order's Archives, the light was as scarce as in the foyer. Tall shelves crammed with hundreds of contraptions, prototypes, maps, and patents filled the massive arched hall. Jasper halted in front of a wall lined up with cabinets packed with iron boxes, their tags visible through the glass doors.

1885, 1886... 1891

He extracted the box and went through the files. Contracts for patents; sketches; finished drawings; funding solicitations.

Nothing unusual.

Let's see another one. 1892. The year of The Golden Griffin.

All the events of that year unfolded in the back of his mind while searching through the papers. The patent of his contraption in Seven Dials. The first sketches of *The Golden Griffin*. Octavia and Chalford Blackwell's funding solicitation for their research in Scotland. His design for the engine pods. The report after the accident.

Yet nothing about the new lifting gas. Not a word anywhere.

The urge to read *The Golden Griffin* papers again made him take out the pile of files.

Only to uncover a thick leather binder on the bottom of the box. He picked it up and read the first page.

Humautomaton. 1890.

Rejected under the seal of the Royal House

Status: Forbidden.

"1890? Then why is this binder here?"

Jasper remembered how the highest tier of the Engineers Order hinted at a new and innovative project which would change the future of England – and, perhaps, the entire world. But he had been too busy with his work to pay attention. Then, they had stopped talking about it, and everyone had forgotten the matter.

He flipped through the pages, his face ashen. As much as he wanted to dismiss it, the thought that the binder in his hands had something to do with *The Golden Griffin* became a sinister foreboding in his mind.

What the hell is this? Humans half turned into automata? Limbs and organs replaced to serve multiple purposes? Was that their idea of outstanding innovation? No wonder the Royal House rejected such a monstrosity! Edmund – Did Edmund know about this?

"Yes, I did. That case brought Carmina to me," Edmund confirmed later, pushing the bookshelf back to cover the patch of flooring that hid the ladder to the underground. "Her Majesty not only rejected the project as unethical, but also asked me to be mindful of the Engineers Order's every move. For a long time after that, Carmina backed me with information from the clients of her establishment. We found nothing. Perhaps Quimby convinced Leythfordham and his supporters that their experiment was pure madness, and they gave up.

"As for how it might be related to what happened to the *Griffin*, don't overthink it. These are different cases, which occurred almost two years distance from one another. In all probability, that explosion's purpose was to get rid of the Blackwells. We need to find out who wanted that and why. Their names have no connection with the Humautomaton experiment. Do not chase dead ends."

9

"I do hope you have a very solid reason to come to my private study at night and risk being seen."

Jasper felt the pointed look of Carmina's green eyes cutting as a piece of glass. It was the most dangerous time for him to be at the Cinnamon Dove, but he had no choice. He couldn't go to Scotland without letting her know.

He held her gaze. "I must leave London for a few days. I might have found something to get us closer to what happened to *The Golden Griffin*. If anything comes up while I'm away, notify Edmund. I assume Hazel used his letter."

Carmina tucked a loose strand of hair behind her ear, her expression more forgiving. "She settled in Leythfordham's household as Amelia Hartling. I trust she will report soon. Tell me about your findings."

"This cannot be a coincidence," she concluded after Jasper briefed her about the two scientists' papers. "Perhaps Quimby had informed some of his peers for whatever reasons. At least one other person besides the Senior Lord must have known about this new gas since before *The Golden Griffin*. Why else would Ivy Blackwell live hidden under a false name in Paris if not for protection? Or why would anyone ransack her house in London? Or want her killed? But we need evidence."

"Hopefully, I shall find it in Scotland.

"One last thing." He stopped, before opening the door to leave. "Edmund didn't release you from service. You are still his agent. My brother only wanted to protect his people. Please, don't hate him."

For one brief moment, he read raw pain in Carmina's eyes.

"Hate Edmund? No, I could never hate him. When are you leaving?"

"Tomorrow at noon."

THE SQUARE-SHAPED BUILDING of the Assignments Office formed a dark spot hidden behind the entrance to the vast expanse of the airharbour. In the distance, the quiet berths signalled a rather scarce activity that night. Which made Jasper's plan much easier.

The guards were still on watch at the gate – and showing them his Engineers Order badge to be granted passage wasn't exactly the best option. Still, he had other means to get in.

He crept along the red brick wall, careful to keep away from the lamp lights, blending with the shadows, until he reached the back of the structure. The only place to climb without being seen.

The small bricks didn't offer much purchase, and the canvas bag on his shoulder only added to the burden. He cursed his unsteady grip and the rubble falling from under his feet.

Jasper looked above and blinked, trying to remove the

small particles of dust that blurred his vision. The top of the wall profiled as a thick red line against the sky.

Almost there.

He gritted his teeth and pushed himself up on the wide edge. The darkness hid him well enough, allowing him to jump down in the tall grass and follow the building wall to the emergency side door.

To open it was the easiest part. He extracted a thin copper pin out of his pocket – his most reliable tool whenever he needed to infiltrate somewhere – and in a matter of minutes disappeared inside Hadrian Hayes' office.

The ledger. Everything that comes and goes through this airharbour is in his ledger.

Hayes had left the register on the desk. A bulky book stained with ink, filled with the clerk's small irregular handwriting. Jasper flipped through the pages until he found the date he wanted.

Wednesday, 19th of June. 1895. The day of *The Skycradle*'s technical inspection.

Among the names of aviators and airharbour engineers, he spotted the information he needed.

The Skycradle

Owner: Mrs Octavia Blackwell.

Custodian: Miss Ivy Theodora Blackwell.

Nature of request: technical inspection.

Total duration: three hours.

Employees detached: Archibald Chancery, Stephen Hayden, Nathaniel Herbert.

Status: external techs, courtesy of Alexis McQuillian, Marquess of Leythfordham, on behalf of the Engineers Order.

He picked up the speakerbox's receiver and dialled Carmina's code.

"Archibald Chancery, Stephen Hayden, Nathaniel

Herbert. Find out everything you can about these men. Leythfordham sent them to the airharbour the other day, using the authority of the Engineers Order. They might have tried to rig Ivy's ship."

~

"PLEASE HAVE mercy on my poor soul, Miss Ivy!" Mrs Carraway pleaded, her hands clasped in a desperate petition. "Going to Scotland alone with His Lordship is inappropriate by all standards. Allow me to come with you!"

Ivy didn't budge an inch.

"I need you to sort out the mess in our house and explain to the constables what happened. We shouldn't take advantage of Lady Hollingsworth's grace for too long. Besides, Jasper is my work partner. So, by the *Reform*'s standards, this trip is *entirely appropriate*. We shall depart tomorrow at noon, as planned."

The yellow light of the electric bulb cast a crude shade on her stern face, highlighting her frowned eyebrows. It was already late after an eventful day, but neither of them wanted to concede.

Ivy was unyielding. She couldn't postpone their research trip. Or leave the house in that state and take Mrs Carraway with them. Travelling alone with Jasper made her more anxious than she was ready to admit. But she had to do it if they wanted to confirm – and use – her parents' discovery.

"If I may, I would love to join your party," Rowena said, standing next to Ivy like an ally against Mrs Carraway. "My reputation should be enough to keep gossip at bay. I would be glad if you could trust me as Miss Blackwell's travel companion."

Ivy turned to her, surprised. Lady Hollingsworth and

Jasper had shown her more kindness in a few days than she had received in an entire year.

"Thank you, Lady Hollingsworth. Your generosity saved me once again."

"I believe you should call me by my name." Rowena smiled and extended her hand to Ivy as a token of their new friendship. "With such company, it will be a most interesting trip. Now tell me, is your cargo hold big enough?"

"What for?"

"For my steammotor. Though I do not use it in London, we shall need it in Scotland."

Ivy looked at her, stunned. She should have imagined that the royal mechanic's household owned one of those steam-powered horseless vehicles on four wheels, capable of moving by themselves with the help of a boiler and a steering lever.

"Yes, it is. But who will drive?"

"Of course, I shall," Rowena said, leaving Ivy once again agape.

~

ROWENA OPENED the inlaid lid of the brass pocket watch hanging from her travel gear's corset.

Half past seven in the morning – enough time to check the steammotor before everyone gathered for breakfast.

Her vehicle was still polished and well maintained, without the slightest trace of dust, sparkling as new. Its long and slender front that hid the boiler seemed a fish ready to take on the waters. The black retractable roof was up, hiding the dark brown leather front seats and the bench in the back.

It was her father's gift to her, which she had stopped using after Jade's death. But, if Jasper could get over his darkest fears and run to the airharbour to help Ivy, she could get over hers and help them both.

They were going to a remote little village in Scotland, where her steammotor would be their only means of transportation. She would drive it, although the painful memory of the day she'd last done that was as clear as a cloudless sky.

Her mind recalled a bright early afternoon in mid-June, three years before. The light summer wind carried the fragrance of the gardens to the stall where she kept her new steammotor. Jasper had taught her how to pilot it, and that day they would drive together before going to the airharbour for *The Golden Griffin*'s first flight.

Jasper took his seat next to her while she put on her goggles and leather gloves. "Let's go to Seven Dials. I want to show you something."

"In St. Giles? Why on Earth should we go to the slums? The place is dangerous, is it not?"

"What slums!" He grinned, watching her press the pedals with the tip of her boot, putting the vehicle in motion after the water in the boiler reached the right temperature. "St. Giles now has sewerage, paved streets, electric lights, and gondotram stations. There are still some courts to avoid, but it has become quite decent."

"Then you want to show me a slum turned into a habitable neighbourhood? The wonders of progress?"

"No, I want to show you my latest work. I want you to be the first to see it."

She sped up, driving with ease past hackneys, mechanical horses, and other steammotors.

"Rowe, you are nothing short of amazing!" Jasper shouted in the wind. "You are officially the tamer of this monster! I doubt another woman in London equals your skill!"

"That is because of my excellent tutor! I am so glad I had you for myself these past days!"

They stopped near an establishment whose rusty wrought iron sign read The Copper Kettle. Jasper's new piece was standing in the middle of the Dials junction, mounted on an iron post. A large sphere made of seven circle-shaped brass dials that intersected and moved in a circular motion, each with its individual axis.

An astounding contraption that was at the same time a compass and a clock.

"Jasper, this is so beautiful!" She looked at the metallic sphere, enthralled by the continuous movement of its circles.

"I made it so that one can see the time and the cardinal directions from all sides. To help the lost ones find their way –"

He stared at her without any other word. The weight of his gaze made her turn her eyes back to the steammotor, in an attempt to return to safer grounds.

Rowena opened the door on the driver's side.

"We should go. We can always come back here later."

She didn't realise back then how right she was.

They drove to the airharbour, where Jasper and the other engineers had to do the final checks before *The Golden Griffin*'s test flight. If everything went well, the airship would soon receive her royal guests.

Jasper stared at the airharbour skyline, which was getting closer and closer. "After we send *The Golden Griffin* to the sky and Jade receives the promotion, I need to tell you something."

Each detail of that evening was still engraved in her mind. The crew disappearing in the gondola. Jade waving at them a few moments later from the observation deck, proud of his assignment as safety officer. Jasper's laugh and his eyes locked on the golden griffin painted on the envelope of the airship, oblivious of everything else.

He would watch from the berth, along with her and her father, Benedict Quimby, and a few other engineers of the Order.

Jade would be promoted, Jasper would see his beloved engines in action, and she would be with him at the most important event of his life. Convincing his twin brother to take his place on the ship wasn't such a terrible idea, after all.

"Send her up!" were Jasper's last words before *The Golden Griffin* retracted her anchorage grapples and took off her deck.

Only to blast less than half an hour later with a thunderous roar, turning into a ball of fire before their eyes.

That was when her world and Jasper's fell apart.

"To own something like this and not use it – I don't understand," Ivy said in awe, tracing the smooth surface of the steammotor with her fingers. They were waiting for the servants to fasten their luggage at the vehicle's rear before they departed for the airharbour.

"You are right. Perhaps I should drive it more often," Rowena replied, with a rather sorrowful look. Her voice seemed distant and sad – as if her mind travelled to some unbeknownst corner of her memory – but Ivy didn't ask. Though she liked Lady Hollingsworth, she intended to stick to her code of conduct, which was to stay away from other people's affairs.

"Time to go," Rowena said over the hiss of the steaming boiler, putting on her driver goggles and leather gloves. "We are ready."

Ivy jumped into the seat next to her. The retractable roof was down, allowing the mild breeze to caress their faces. She intended to enjoy every minute of the ride and forget about her troubles for the time being.

"Rats and caterpillars, this is incredible!" Ivy shouted. "I never imagined a steammotor was like this! Or that the ladies of the *ton* take driving lessons!"

Rowena offered a restrained smile. "They do not. My father gave me this motor, and I wanted to drive it myself. Jasper taught me how. Three years ago."

Three years ago – that bloody moment in time none of them could forget.

The buzz and hum of the steam engine soothed her, emptying her mind. Soon enough, the red brick building of the Airharbour Assignments Office took shape in front of them.

JASPER WAS SITTING on a leather-covered bench in *The Skycradle*'s gondola, his boots propped on the railing and his hands under his head, as he waited for Ivy.

His plan to sneak into her airship had worked, allowing him to find further evidence about Leythfordham – and watch the sunrise from amidst the airharbour.

He closed his eyes, recalling the motley scenery of the early morning – the sun casting shades of red and orange on the airships, covering them in an ethereal glow; the industrious clamour of the crafts coming and going, blending with the loud voices shouting commands from the berths; the sooty odours of oil and metal.

That hubbub reminded him of his love for the airharbour and everything in it.

An unusual roar made him stand up and look over the railing, only to freeze in place. He rushed to Ivy's pilot seat and put on her goggles to make sure that what he saw wasn't the product of his tired brain.

Rowena's steammotor, with Rowena behind the steering lever and Ivy grinning next to her was indeed as real as his presence in *The Skycradle*.

"Let down the cargo hold hatch!" Ivy instructed while standing and waving, her bright red hair a messy loose ponytail over her shoulder. "We're coming in!"

Jasper ran to the command board, dumbfounded, his face ghastly white. He understood how hard it must have been for Rowena to pilot that steammotor again. While they kept deep in their hearts the memory of their last day of carefree happiness, neither of them had dared to talk about it again after Jade's death.

He climbed the ladder to the cargo hold, where Rowena was guiding her steammotor over the ramp. As soon as she got off the vehicle, he clutched her shoulders, searching for a sign of anguish in her eyes.

"Why? You could have provided a carriage for her. Are you all right?"

"I am perfectly fine, while you are perfectly rude," Rowena said, with a reprimanding squint. "What happened to your manners?"

Jasper turned to Ivy, extending his hand.

"Forgive me, I was inconsiderate," he said apologetically. "I have no excuse for my incivility, but I assure you there were good reasons that made me act first and think later."

"We all have our share of oddities." Ivy dismissed him with a short wave of her hand. "What we need now, though, is some help with our luggage."

"Our luggage?" an astonished Jasper repeated, while

unfastening the two cases from the steammotor's luggage compartment.

"I shall join you in Scotland. My maid has asked the cottage keeper to prepare an extra room," Rowena said. "Tell me, how did you plan to move around there? Flying the airship over the villages, perhaps?"

Jasper laughed, understanding Rowena's decision. It was not to help Ivy, as he'd believed, but him as well. Impulsively, he crushed her slender figure in an embrace. Steammotor aside, with a companion for Ivy, he could search for clues with no question asked.

"Thank you." He released her, his blue eyes sparkling with gratitude.

~

"NEXT TIME we go to Scotland, remind me to take the bloody train!" Ivy was struggling to keep *The Skycradle* steady on her navigation course in the fierce wind. "It's a wonder we are still on the right coordinates!"

"And we shall remain so," Jasper said, as unfazed as she was agitated.

Standing next to her, he was helping her navigate through the storm, guiding the airship through the air currents. It was almost evening, and the weather had delayed them by at least an hour. The rain blocked their long-distance vision, knocking ceaselessly into the windows.

Ivy was in a foul mood, and Jasper's attitude only added fuel to the fire. She knew every nook and cranny of her ship, her every whim and caprice. Yet she couldn't have piloted her without Jasper, who was as impassive as a tombstone, as sure of his skills as she was of her airship.

That made her appear like a mere apprentice as compared to him – which she didn't like at all.

She also kept thinking about the strange scene from earlier – an intense personal moment between two people who shared a history.

Your employer happens to be my close friend, Jasper had said. Now she was sure it was more than that. But she refrained from peeking any further or wondering about what bound them. Though it was hard to ignore the ache in her heart at that closeness, which she had never shared with anyone.

"Start the descent," Jasper said. "I'm trying to find a suitable place for anchorage."

Which proved to be harder than they anticipated. A vast stretch of hills, water streams and bushy plateaus unfolded below – none of them suitable for fixing anchorage grapples.

In that desolate expanse, somewhere between Muirkirk and Glenbuck, the cottage was the only sign of human touch. Surrounded by a thick small stone fence, with a water thread winding in front of the wooden gate, the place resembled a farm. Its grey sturdy stones and roof added to the general gloom.

"Rats and caterpillars, what anchorage! We are in the middle of blasted nowhere! With nothing we can call a berth!"

"Over there!" Jasper pointed towards a stony outcrop close to the cottage. "That plateau is also flat enough to drive the steammotor out of the cargo hold."

"You can't be serious! You want me to land *there*? Will it even hold?"

"An aviator cannot expect only fine weather, well-organised airharbours and smooth berths," Jasper said. He was harsh, but she couldn't blame him – she had done little else but complain, for almost the entire duration of their flight. "If you have a better idea, I shall be delighted to hear it."

Ivy didn't reply. Instead, she docked *The Skycradle* and stopped the engines. By the time they reached the cottage, they were soaked to the bone.

"Miss Blackwell, Your Ladyship, Your Lordship, hurry!" The old servant was waiting with the door open, beckoning them in. "Reckon you need a hot bath and some rest after journeying in this foul weather."

"Aye," Jasper said, leaving the two suitcases on the floor. "I wouldn't mind some kidney pie and ale either. I am so hungry I could eat a whole herd."

10

The downpour had stopped, yet the clouds still loomed thick and grey over the rugged hills, as daylight slowly faded into a bleak dusk. In the distance, green patches of bushes resembled small dark shadows spread across a colourless landscape.

It felt miles away from the civilised world. A train station in the middle of nowhere for three neighbouring towns stood as the only visible sign of technology. Barren land, unwelcoming hills, and mucky trails shaped the surroundings.

Ivy and Rowena had retired for the evening, too tired to question Jasper's decision to go to nearby Glenbuck. To secure the mine gas they needed for their experiment, he'd said. They didn't need to know his ulterior motives. Over the casual dinner conversation, Mrs Cormack, the housekeeper, had provided plenty of information. Which he intended to put to good use.

"I reckon many things have changed since the Blackwells used to work here, ain't it so?" Jasper had asked with an innocent smile while stuffing his face with kidney pie. "Three years is quite a long time."

"Some did, some did not," the housekeeper said. "The lads in the colliery still drink their minds at the Broken Wagon. But strange things started happening two or three years ago. They are mining and delivering coal all over England. Yet, my husband saw with 'is own two eyes carts full of mine gas tanks leaving in the dead of night once in a few months. Where and why – nobody can tell. That McAvery is up to no good. Always doing shady business and picking at people."

"Who is that?" Jasper asked, seemingly to keep the conversation going.

"The colliery overseer. Does a good job, but Shane Gilford – the owner – tries to keep him at a distance. No wonder, since McAvery would sell 'is mother for a few coins. There is some bad blood between them as of late."

Jasper didn't believe in coincidences, much less when they involved transporting mine gas illegally around the time of *The Golden Griffin* incident.

"Another change is that nobody ever comes to these villages anymore," Mrs Cormack said, with a trace of sadness in her voice. "When Mrs Octavia and Mr Chalford lived here – God rest their souls – quite a few people from London used to cross our doorstep. I still keep the record of those visits."

"The record of those visits?" Ivy asked, with her fork in mid-air and a baffled expression on her face. "You were keeping a record of my parents' guests? Why?"

"Oh, but your parents requested it, Miss Ivy. You weren't in England, so I had no idea where to send the ledger after their death. I brought it with me today. I reckon you want to see who their friends were, ain't it so?"

Jasper didn't find anything amiss in the ledger. Ivy's

parents were among the most famous scientists in England. A lot of influential people came to check how they were faring and how their experiments were going.

Most visits were from Benedict Quimby – which was only natural since he was the Senior Lord of the Engineers Order and their main sponsor.

The last page had only one record.

Edmund Asher, Earl of Wyverstone, with Lady Emmeline Rexworth Asher. Arrived on Wednesday, 25th of May. Left on Friday, 27th of May. 1892.

His brother had been the last one to call on the Blackwells, one week before they left for Paris and about two weeks before *The Golden Griffin*. But Edmund hadn't been aware of the two scientists' discovery. He wondered how many of those who came there actually knew the truth about their research.

Jasper found the Broken Wagon easily. A run-down building with dirty windows and a thick wooden door, sporting the iron sign of a cart that had lost two of its four wheels. If by design or they had fallen off, Jasper couldn't say.

He entered the shabby establishment, attracting everyone's attention. In such a place, where everyone knew everyone, a stranger was always looked upon with curious, often hostile eyes.

Good. Jasper took a seat at a small table in a corner. *Now come at me.*

The smell of smoke and cheap tobacco blended with a foul odour of dirty clothes, sweat and stale ale, in a heavy and cheerless atmosphere.

People didn't come there to drink for pleasure. That was a place where they drank to forget.

"Who are ye and what's yer business 'ere?" A bald man in his late forties took a seat at his table, looking at him with suspicious eyes. He was tall and muscled, and his sleeves were rolled up to reveal his heavily tattooed arms. "Better be convincing, else I'll throw ye to the dogs. Ye with the airship from earlier?"

"That I am," Jasper said, undaunted. "I came with Her Ladyship the Duchess of Craigshollow. I am her driver."

"Duchess of what? Never 'eard of that. Ye better be telling the truth."

I'm not, but you don't have to know that.

"I am. Her Ladyship and His Lordship the duke lived in America for many years, doing business, instead of living in England, doing nothing, like other noblemen. Their wealth has tripled since."

"What this Duchess of Crang–whatever wants with our town?" The other man was still sceptical, but Jasper could detect a sparkle of interest in his voice.

"She wanted to see a bit of Scotland, so she rented an airship and came here. While I am looking to secure a deal for His Lordship."

"What would that be?"

"I'm afraid that is something I can only tell overseer McAvery."

"I'm the overseer," he said, equally pleased and surprised. "I'm all ears."

"While in America, His Lordship became interested in mine gas. He found some new uses for it and wants to expand his business. The duke is considering buying some nice quantities from the Glenbuck mine."

"This is a colliery, not a gas mine," the tattooed man said pointedly. "Go somewhere else."

"A wealthy man like my master has excellent information sources. He wanted a contract with a gas mine and chose this one. However, he found out that the owner already had another customer. I need to know who is that customer so that His Lordship can prepare a better offer."

"Listen, lad. I don't know what ye're talkin' 'bout. Leave now and spit yer nonsense somewhere else. If I still find ye here –"

Jasper put a pouch full of coins on the table before he could finish his threat.

"You know as well as I that Shane Gilford is selling cartloads of gas tanks. Likewise, you know as well as I that this colliery makes its money, its *real* money, out of that. I want to know *who* is buying all that gas.

"This is only a small upfront payment," Jasper said, while the man weighed the coins in his hand. "I want one gas tank tomorrow, as a token of the deal. If you find out the information I want, I'll give you another one. If my master secures the deal, you will fare even better. It's in your best interest to help me."

"What makes ye think I'd trust a stranger?"

The way you looked at that pouch of coins. Mrs Cormack was right. You'd sell your mother for money, you rotten bastard.

"You strike me as a practical man who can recognise an opportunity when he sees one. Needless to say, this matter requires utmost secrecy."

"Ye have some guts, lad, I ought to give ye credit for that." The man laughed, pleased. "Come tomorrow morning at the colliery and ask for Ichabod McAvery. I'll prepare your gas tank."

"What about the other thing? Will you tell me what I need to know? Who is your master's business partner? Who is receiving all those gas tanks?"

The moment of heavy silence that followed seemed an hour.

"Only Gilford knows that. But I'll find out by tomorrow

night." He dangled the pouch of coins under Jasper's nose. "Just make sure ye bring another fat lass like this one."

~

"Why must I stay here while you are having all the fun?" Ivy wailed. "It isn't fair by any blasted standards!"

"Because we don't want to attract unwanted attention or make anyone suspect we have *any* connection with Octavia and Chalford Blackwell. That is a bloody *colliery*, not Hyde Park, so I fail to see the fun. I'm taking Rowena with me for reasons I have already explained. She is the Duchess of Craigshollow, and I'm her driver. That place can be dangerous, and I'm not sure I can protect both of you."

"I don't need protection! I'm coming with you!"

"Please, be reasonable." Jasper was losing his patience. His tone was edgy and abrupt. "I secured with great difficulty that gas tank we need. If McAvery sniffs I lied, we might return empty-handed – which means we shall not be able to do any experiment. Or even worse, we might not return at all."

"All right, I give up!" Ivy raised her arms in resignation. "You two go, and I will explore the workshop."

Jasper let out a sigh of relief. He was anxious enough to have Rowena with him in that place. Both women would have been too much. He had told them only a part of the story, omitting the other piece of information he had requested from the overseer.

He only needed Rowena to play her role well as the Duke of Craigshollow's wife asking for the gas tank in her husband's name. Her presence would suffice to make that man believe his story.

Soon, he was driving on the dirt road to Glenbuck. Next to him, Rowena was staring at the desolate surroundings.

"Forgive me," he said, glancing at her. "For making you lie for me. For all the compromises you accepted for my sake."

"It's all right." A smile brightened her face. "It's just – I realised how I missed it. The two of us together like this. I miss those times."

Jasper looked at her again, the unexpected words startling him. Rowena usually kept her feelings to herself, yet she had gathered her courage to speak. That raw, clumsy confession echoed his soul.

"I haven't forgotten that day," he said. "I never would. That was the last time I was truly happy. And it was because of you."

Her eyes told him it was her turn to be startled, but they arrived at the colliery before she could answer.

The place was grim and covered in black dust, made of an assortment of brick outbuildings, pit entrances and wooden scaffolds. The air was heavy with the smell of soot and coal. People swarmed by, pushing loaded carts, pulling strings, and pressing lift levers to get the workers to and from the underground.

"We are looking for Ichabod McAvery," Jasper said to a collier who was staring in turns at Rowena and the steammotor. "I reckon you can let him know we're here."

McAvery emerged from a small building nearby, eyeing Rowena with a look Jasper didn't like at all.

"Good morning Yer Ladyship," he said in a coarse voice, raising a corner of his mouth in a mockery of a smile. "Yer husband must be a fool to let such a woman wonder by 'erself in places like this."

"Mr McAvery, I advise you to mind your manners." Rowena's sharp tone could cut through a rock. "I am here on my husband's behalf. If he is pleased with your services, he will reward you well. But one word from me and any deal is off."

McAvery didn't reply, turning to Jasper instead.

"Yer tank is in that barrel over there, lad." He pointed towards a young man who was rolling a small barrel to the steammotor. "Ye came here to buy coal, understood? Speak to anyone about the gas, and I'll kill ye with my own hands."

"Worry not," Jasper said quickly, seeing Rowena turn pale. "Secrecy is in everyone's best interest."

McAvery nodded knowingly, while his men secured the barrel inside the steammotor. Jasper helped Rowena into her seat.

"Have you found out?" he asked, before getting into the steammotor. "The piece of information I requested?"

"Come tonight at the Broken Wagon. Bring the money, and ye'll have yer answer."

THE WORKSHOP they'd seen the night before in the far corner of the house was only a cover for her parents' actual working space. Ivy moved a cupboard full of tools aside and pushed the stained wall behind it, revealing a narrow passage leading to an underground cellar.

She opened the laboratory door, displaying a triumphant grin when she noticed Jasper's amazement. It had taken her a while to discover the place, but it was worth the effort.

The only connection of the laboratory with the exterior was a network of tubular ventilation pipes that covered the ceiling, which aired the room and emptied through small vents outside, at the ground level. Though dim, the electric light of the bulbs mounted in the raw brick walls revealed the interior well enough.

Containers, valves, pipes, sieves, and gauges merged into an undistinguishable maze. They'd seen them in the two scientists' drawings, but the real thing was more confusing and complicated than Ivy had imagined.

"Given my father's inclination towards hidden spaces, I was certain I would find something like this here," Ivy said, watching Jasper set up the gas evaluation machine. Her university in Paris had a few such devices, but she had never worked with one. Judging from the ease with which he handled it, he had. "I don't think many people knew about this place, Mrs Cormack included. The workshop upstairs was sparkling clean, while this one was drowned in dust, so I had to make it usable. I searched for other papers my parents might have left here, but I only found old books, empty phials, and bottles of substances. No letter, no note, nothing."

"You couldn't possibly think your parents were that careless as to leave their work in such a remote corner of England."

"Then how can we handle this installation without a proper explanation? My parents' notes and drawings aren't enough for us to understand what's in this room. I'm an aviator. I pilot airships, and I know a lot about them. But I'm no chemist. Neither are you."

"Neither were your parents if I'm not mistaken. And yet, they discovered a new lifting gas, created their own gas separation laboratory, and conducted all the work for *The Golden Griffin* from here. Shouldn't that be enough of an incentive to you?"

"They had help." Ivy spread the plans they brought from London on the empty table close to the weird installation that filled most of the room. "Two chemist friends of theirs from Sweden. We have no one."

"But we have their work, which is the most important thing. We only need to do what your parents wrote and be careful. Pressurising mine gas is not a safe procedure. I hope you are aware of that."

"I am," she said. "But I wouldn't miss this for anything."

She opened a cabinet and took out gloves, goggles, and leather masks to cover their noses and mouths.

Jasper uncapped the gas tank, careful to tighten its opening at the base of the first container. He pressed the first side lever, and the gauges came to life with a powerful wheeze.

"First, we shall get rid of the carbon dioxide and the heavier components," Jasper said, his voice muffled by the mask. "Which we should collect in here."

He pointed to the first vessel of the installation, a metal barrel connected to the pipe. Ivy stared at the gauges without understanding too much of what was happening. She never considered chemistry her favourite thing, and she hadn't bothered to check her parents' drawings and explanations on the matter.

"We passed the first stage." Jasper disengaged and sealed the collecting container when the dial needle turned back to zero. "Now we should extract the methane to purify it further."

He looked at the drawings again, then pressed the second lever. A hiss, a brief movement of the dial needle, then the installation came to a halt.

"Is anything wrong?" Ivy asked, suddenly apprehensive.

"I am not sure. While I do understand the process, as you said, I am no chemist. I am only following your parents' instructions." Jasper took off his gloves and traced the handwriting and drawings with his finger, without finding any new piece of information that could help.

"What are the required conditions for the second stage to start?" Ivy asked, frowning at the installation. "As I understand, we need to process the remaining gas. The dials indicate it is in the right container, so why is nothing happening?"

Jasper stood motionless for a few moments, then clasped her shoulders, smiling brightly.

"Ivy, you might not be skilled in chemistry, but you surely know how to ask the right questions! It is indeed in the right container, but I think I got a parameter wrong. The *only* condition for the gas to reach stage two is to pass stage one completely. Which means to be entirely purified of carbon dioxide. If nothing happens, it must be because there are carbon dioxide residues in the remaining gas. I must have disengaged the duct too quickly!"

"Then we must start all over again?" Ivy's expression was as worried as Jasper's was happy. "We only got one gas tank. What if we fail again?"

"Worry not, this time we shall do it right. But first we need to release the remaining gas from the installation. Thank heavens for these masks and the ventilation system on the ceiling!"

The process proved long and complicated, each step splitting the mine gas further, sealing the components into their correspondent containers along the way. Neither of them knew if it was night or day when they collected the purified gas into the last and smallest brass container and released it into the gas evaluation machine.

The needles on the gauges danced back and forth before their eyes until they finally stopped.

"Lighter than air, colourless, odourless, and it does not

react. We have our answer." Jasper wiped his forehead with the back of his hand. "If we replicate your parents' installation at a factory scale, we can use it for airships. Our laevium is real."

~

"GOOD!" McAvery's eyes were sparkling with an almost feral light when Jasper put another pouch of coins on the table. "I am a man of my word meself. I 'ave what ye asked. I stole the deed for the last delivery, which was a few months ago. See for yerself. But I ought to bring it back, else Gilford will find out and be on alert."

Jasper snatched the paper from his hand.

"It's a woman from London," the overseer said. "'er name is Emmeline Rexworth Asher."

11

"Please be careful with those glass phials!" Rowena instructed, supervising the unloading of the cart and the transportation of the goods into her new school.

"Aye, aye, Yer Ladyship!"

Jack Killen placed the last crate on his shoulder. His children, eager to assist, carried books, pens, and inkwells.

"Lady Rowena, ain't you scared? What if someone is after you?"

"Shhhh! Blake, I told you, that is our little secret. No one but you and I must know!"

Her voice was no more than a whisper, afraid that someone else besides Jack's son might hear.

She had been lucky to have only little Blake with her two days before, when she'd found the driver's door of her steammotor smeared with letters painted in red.

LEAVE IF YE VALUE YER LIFE

I must not worry about such a tasteless prank. It means nothing.

Rowena followed everyone into the building, halting on the doorstep to take in the view.

The interior was freshly washed and painted, with sparkling clean windows. Large retractable tables were mounted into the walls. The cabinets contained all the necessary supplies for the activities of such establishment. The place even had electric light and a speakerbox – which was rare for a former warehouse.

She had no reason to worry. At the start of the following week, she would open its doors.

"Ve're done 'ere, Yer Ladyship!" one of the workers said with a satisfied grin. "I daresay dis place never looked better!"

"Thank you, Hector! And good luck with your work at the new factory!"

Then she turned to the others, her face beaming. "That would be enough for today. Please come collect your pay. For later, I have ordered dinner for everyone at the Copper Kettle."

She joined her helpers outside. The day was cloudy, but their cheerful mood compensated for that bleak end of the week. It was still early, so calling on Jasper at the workshop was a tempting idea. She hadn't seen him for almost a week, since their return from Glenbuck.

Rowena started her steammotor's boiler and waited.

In the late afternoon stillness, a deafening roar reverberated from the nearby skystation in Holborn, suppressing the gurgle of the water reaching its boiling point.

Everyone's gaze turned to the suspended tracks.

It was as if a tremendous thunder had descended from the sky, cracking the earth to its very core.

"What in the Lord's name was that!" a frightened woman shrieked. "Hurry! To the skystation!"

A moment later, the area in front of the school emptied. Men, women, and children ran in the direction of the dreadful noise.

Rowena pressed the pedals of her steammotor and followed.

It took her only a few minutes to get to the skystation, ahead of everyone else. She stopped, petrified. In her mind, her old school in ruins was the most frightening scene she could ever witness.

She had been horribly mistaken.

~

JASPER PUT his pen down and stared at the sheet of paper that covered almost half of his workbench, displaying the dissected body of the gondola.

Ivy traced his drawing with her finger. "This will be the first airship with such a heating system. Now I understand why you became a member of the Engineers Order at such a young age. Your idea might work."

"The heat will come through a bidirectional structure," Jasper said. "Below the floor, we will set up a hot water pipe network. The water will circulate underneath the entire surface and will be pumped up by this device whose purpose is to create pressure and boil the water.

"Then we have the upper part." He moved his hand over the small fans placed into the airship's gondola walls. "The steam will act upon this ventilation system, producing hot air to heat the interior."

"The airship will use laevium as lifting gas, so it is safe from any explosion risk," Ivy said. "Now that we have the engines, ventilation, and heating system in place, we can proceed with drawing the design and making the scale model. I have some ideas."

"We should leave them for tomorrow." Jasper rolled up

the large drawing of the airship's innards. "Let us call it a day and take you home."

"Much as I like the Hollingsworth mansion, it is not my home," Ivy said. "More than a week has passed, and I still can't move back to my house. The Hollingsworth family's coachman takes me here each morning, and you bring me back each evening. Had I been a lady from your circles, I would have thought you are courting me, but I am aware this is not the case. What are you hiding from me?"

Jasper looked at her, alert. Had he been that obvious? He couldn't tell her the truth, but he had to give her some explanation.

"I hide nothing from you." He tried to reassure her, but Ivy's only answer was a doubtful stare. "You are working with me, and I must make sure you are safe. Need I remind you that a band of hoodlums have just ransacked your house?"

Ivy opened her mouth to reply, but the metallic chime of the speakerbox cut off her words. Jasper turned to his desk in surprise. That particular sound announced only one person, and he didn't hear it too often.

Reluctantly, he picked up the receiver.

"It's me," he said, awaiting the imminent disaster. "What happened?"

"Master Hollingsworth's coachman is on his way to take Miss Blackwell home," Edmund said, his voice cold and collected at the other end of the line. "After she leaves, go to the skystation in Holborn to do a technical investigation. A gondotram full of people has just fallen off its track, and I need to find out why. I shall arrange for you to present your full report the day after tomorrow at the emergency assembly of the Engineers Order. But be careful about what you say there. Play stupid if need be. I don't trust half of that lot."

~

Making his way through the crowd gathered around the skystation proved to be a rather challenging undertaking for Jasper. A bizarre blend of nurses, constables and onlookers were running around, barking orders or just gawking at the horrifying scene.

Stretchers, blankets, bandages, and medicine covered the entire place. The air stank of blood and disinfectant. A few braver bystanders who had volunteered to help the nurses were separating the dead bodies from the survivors, putting severed limbs aside, and dressing screaming patients' wounds.

The skystation had halted all operations. No one had access to the tracks.

"Clear the area! Clear the area!" The policemen tried to push the crowd aside, but to no avail. "Make way for the helpers!"

In the general chaos, Jasper noticed Rowena's steammotor, and his eyes looked for her frantically. She was with the nurses, cleaning a woman's wound, her pale blue dress dirty and smeared with blood, and her face ashen.

Much as he wished to comfort her, it felt inappropriate amidst all that agony. Besides, he had his own matters to take care of.

He strode purposefully towards the group of constables who were struggling to keep everyone away from the gondotram wreck.

"I am Jasper Kendall Asher of Her Majesty's Engineers Order. I require passage for the technical investigation of this incident." He showed them his badge. The small golden cogwheel engraved with the initials of the Order and his name prompted the constables to step aside.

He climbed the deformed carcass of the wagon to inspect the giant cogwheels that used to thrust it on the tracks. They couldn't have broken so easily. The gripping system was sturdy and safe and should have held well.

The main cog check gave him the answer. Every wagon included a blocking mechanism that triggered automatically should the cogwheels go astray. There, it was missing. The four bars holding the system in place were cut off, preventing the cogwheels from blocking.

In all probability, someone interfered with the gondotram on purpose.

"Have you found something, sir? With so much to do for those poor people, nobody had time to check why this tragedy happened."

The familiar voice drew his attention. Carmina Harcourt was standing at the base of the contorted mass of metal. Dressed as a nurse, her violet hair hidden underneath the white cap, and her features changed by the makeup, she once again reminded him why Edmund called her the queen of disguise.

Jasper jumped off the wreck.

"Someone severed the blocking trigger of the cogwheels," he said, after making sure they were out of earshot. The pile of deformed iron marked as off limits to everyone provided them enough cover to talk.

"It strikes me as odd that it happened so close to Lady Hollingsworth's first school," Carmina said. "Both incidents occurred in the same area. What could have made a building and a gondotram fall without a blast, and with no apparent reason? The gondotram was rigged. I trust your judgement. But why did it fall *here*? And not at Blackfriars or a different skystation?"

They looked at each other, suddenly aware of the answer Jasper had been looking for in the past few weeks.

"If we exclude the possibility of a blast or an earthquake, then it must be *something* hidden *underground*." Jasper's voice shivered with horror. "Something so powerful that its shockwaves took down a building. However, as Edmund always says, we cannot act based on assumptions. We need solid evidence. Let us go down there and find out what it is."

"The only way I can think of is the sewerage tunnels. It will be a stinky but necessary business. I shall meet you after midnight at the old school."

"I wonder how the marquess' wish for a new airharbour is related to what happened here," Jasper said. "Emmeline might be involved as well. But no matter how hard I try to find something on her, I fail. She is as slippery as a fish. I have nothing except that bloody deed in her name."

"I found nothing either. She only called on her lady friends and attended public events and her usual charities. Hazel sent me the names of those who visited Leythfordham in the past two weeks. None of them had any connection to Lady Emmeline Asher."

"Keep tailing her. We need more than one paper with her name on it."

"Leave that to me and my girls. Ginger is now in Glenbuck. I instructed her to find any document related to your sister-in-law. Now I think you would be interested in knowing I traced those three men you've asked about. Archibald Chancery, Stephen Hayden, and Nathaniel Herbert."

"It took you a while."

"That is because they are not engineers, and I followed the wrong path searching for them in the Engineers Order's records. They are not mechanics, but blokes from

Whitechapel who took daily jobs at the docks. They have disappeared without a trace. If we are to believe their wives, they found work at some new factory. But they left in the dead of night and the factory is impossible to locate."

"I keep hearing about that new factory as of late," Jasper said. "Many people in this neighbourhood left like that. Their families receive their wages, with no other detail. However, I'm afraid this case is more than just about finding work. If Leythfordham paid them to rig Ivy's airship, he might have wanted to get rid of them."

~

THE CROWD around the Holborn skystation had increased in the last few hours. People swarmed to see if the news about the terrible accident – which was spreading like wildfire throughout London – was true.

No one else from the Engineers Order appeared. Which meant that Edmund had obtained Quimby's approval for Jasper's assignment as the delegate in charge of the technical investigation.

His work done, Jasper's only thought was to see how Rowena was coping with the disaster. He found her just when she was about to get into her steammotor.

"Jasper –" she whispered, her eyes showing how much the sight of him comforted her. They were so used to be each other's support in the past three years that they needed no words.

When he pulled her to him, she started sobbing, hidden in the safe shelter of his chest.

"I'm sorry you had to go through all this. I'm so sorry, Rowe –"

"I must go." Her eyes met his, her hands still clutching the white cotton of his shirt, wet with her tears. "I let them use my school as a hospital for the time being. It is close from here and large enough to accommodate everyone. Will you come with me?"

Jasper caressed her wet face. "I would come with you to the other side of the world if you asked."

The scene was terrifying even for him, who was no stranger to violence. Yet, as shaken as she was, she had kept her composure while helping the others. His mind went back to the days when she followed him into the gin bars of St. Giles and other establishments by no means fit for a woman, only to drag him out, neglecting her safety. She was recklessly brave, the most selfless woman he had ever met.

Long past sunset, with the outside crowd scattered and all the nurses and patients settled in the makeshift hospital, Jasper drove the steammotor to the Hollingsworth mansion, Rowena already asleep beside him. She never let her guard down like that, she never seemed so fragile and vulnerable, and he felt a fierce need to protect her.

A corner of his lips curled in a rueful smile, thinking about how things had changed since their first encounter. How annoyed he had been with the fourteen-year-old girl who had burst into his master's library all those years ago.

In a ruffled navy dress, her hair a cascade of raven curls over her shoulders, she was as radiant as a summer day. Only that he was a fifteen-year-old boy who had just started as Theophilus Hollingsworth's apprentice. Anything unrelated to his work was an irritating disturbance.

"I heard Jade's brother was here, so I *had* to meet him!" she said, her intense hazel eyes locked on Jasper. "He was right. You are nothing like him. He is as blond and bright as the sun, while you look so dark and brooding. You *are* twins, are you not?"

"Rowena, my dear, not all twins are identical," Master Hollingsworth explained, embarrassed. "And this is not how a young lady enters a room where gentlemen are talking."

"Oh, please forgive me. I shall go. I rushed here and left Jade waiting for me in the garden. Jasper, will you be joining us?"

"I am here to learn, not to play with little girls. If Jade enjoys wasting his time, do not assume I am as shallow as him."

He was harsh, but he meant every word. It had taken two years for his master to accept him. The apprenticeship was more important to him than anything.

Yet there he was, years later, still beside the woman the little girl of that day had become.

His heart trembled at the distant memory, and his gaze drifted to her sleeping face. She was painfully beautiful, the slender fingers of her left hand spread over her blue dress, a loose curl of her hair fallen over her cheek, her chest heaving peacefully in the rhythm of her breathing.

He reached for her slightly parted lips but forced himself back to reality. In their situation, he could offer nothing more than friendship.

THE RUINS of Rowena's former school made a rather sinister meeting point in the empty neighbourhood. Everyone was still drinking at the Copper Kettle and debating upon the events of the day or had long gone to sleep. The streetlamps were broken, and the dim light of the moon was casting strange shadows on the cobblestones. Ever since the building collapsed, people avoided the area after dark. It had an uncanny and foreboding aura.

In the eerie silence, Jasper's instincts were wide awake and alert. He sensed Carmina right before she materialised out of nowhere next to him. Wearing breeches, knee-high boots, and a cap to hide her hair, one could have mistaken her for a young gentleman seeking to discover the mysteries of St. Giles.

"I have the underground map," she said. "One of the entrances to the sewerage tunnels is close from here, between the public baths and the former workhouse. I hope you brought some light. We are going to need it."

Jasper produced a palm-size torch from his pocket. He had been right to trust her obsession for maps. As she had been right to trust his for devices and contraptions. Together, they would find their way. Only that they had no clue about what was waiting at its end.

They started for the point Carmina indicated to begin their search. The workhouse had been closed for over five years, and the area was derelict, excluded from the last significant public works project.

It had been a massive undertaking that redesigned the buildings, terracing them on elevated platforms nearby the gondotram tracks, paved all the alleys and courts, and installed streetlamps in all St. Giles, turning the slums into decent places.

That small corner was a harsh reminder of London before the Reform, before the Engineers Order's technological developments had changed the city.

"There's nothing here." Carmina spread out a scroll on the pavement. "If we are to trust this bloody map, the entrance should have been in this spot. Yet, there is no trace of it."

"Maybe the map is not accurate or is too old. Or the entrance wasn't intended to be discovered too easily." Jasper stared at the buildings of the abandoned workhouse that were looming in the darkness. "This place was left to ruin for a reason."

Without waiting for her answer, he jumped inside through a broken window with the agility of a cat. Carmina had no choice but to follow him.

Inside, the silence was even more oppressive, their light footsteps reverberating with an ominous cadence. They crossed the corridor, trying to determine their surroundings. The working halls were empty, and the sleeping quarters beyond the collapsed doors revealed rusty bedframes covered in dust, broken tables, and pieces of glass from the shattered windows.

Nothing broke the stillness. The entire place seemed frozen.

"Do you think this has anything to do with the Humautomaton experiment?"

Carmina stopped at Jasper's sudden question, turning towards him. "You know about that? No one but me and Edmund worked on that case. We closed it five years ago."

"I found the file while searching in the Engineers Order's archives. Edmund thought the *Griffin* and Humautomaton were distinct matters. However, I am not at all sure about that."

"Edmund's judgement is correct," she said. "Back then, Leythfordham was the strongest supporter of that project. However, he is too much of a coward to keep going after the Queen forbid the Engineers Order to pursue that abomination. Disobeying Her Majesty's order would endanger his position. He would not risk that."

"What if another member of the Order would?"

"Highly unlikely. Not many people knew about that experiment. And not many people have such power in the

Order. Leythfordham is the most influential member, but he is a coward. Quimby is struggling to keep a decent relation between the Order and the Royal House. He wouldn't do something as foolish as defying the Queen."

They reached the end of the corridor which opened onto the central courtyard.

Carmina caught Jasper's arm. "Wait. The place might be guarded."

"I doubt it." Jasper took one tentative step outside. "If this is the entrance to the underground, placing guards in such a visible spot would be an idiotic move."

The moment he got into the square, a sharp bark, followed by a pair of black hounds, stopped him. The dogs revealed their fangs with murderous intent.

One of them jumped at Jasper's chest, throwing him to the ground. He had one second to retaliate and grasp the beast's throat, keeping it at an agonisingly close distance from his face.

The sound of Carmina's pistol resonated twice before both dogs fell in an awkward position, their mouths and eyes wide open, and all four legs stretched. He recognised that reaction. It was the paralysis pistol he made for her years ago. It could disable its target or be lethal, depending on how she used it.

"Blimey Jasper, whatever is wrong with you? Being off duty for so long made you too careless! One more stunt like that and you compromise our mission."

"We should search and find where those beasts came from. Such hounds cannot be stray dogs. They were trained to kill."

"I am not sure that would be wise," Carmina said. "If someone heard those dogs, we might expect a welcome committee we do not wish. We cannot take such a risk when our only weapon is my paralysis pistol!"

"Carmina, when did you become such a coward? As I recall, you never had any problem infiltrating the most unlikely and dangerous places in the past."

He went straight to the open grilled gate mounted into one of the interior walls of the courtyard. The only way to enter was to crawl on all fours. It resembled a narrow tunnel, but the thick darkness made it impossible to see where it was leading.

Jasper lit up the torch, only to reveal a short passage with a dead end.

"They must have come from somewhere else," he said. "Perhaps from somewhere inside these buildings. This is not the entrance to the sewers."

"Feel free to take my reasoning for cowardice, but we are going back *now*. Someone might be already looking for us, and we don't want to be here when those dogs start barking again. We must make do with this scrap of information for the moment. At least we know for sure something is here." Carmina returned to the dark corridor of the main building. "Next time, we are coming with a proper map – which I shall steal tomorrow at the duke's birthday ball. Change of plans. I shall get into that house myself. While you search for clues to incriminate that rotten bastard, I search for the map in his father's library. We shall meet in Leythfordham's private study to compare our findings."

Unlike the son, the duke of Litchborough had been one of the best engineers of his time. He had been among those who planned the sewerage system underneath London. Carmina was right. If a map of that web of tunnels existed, it would be in his house.

12

"The passenger deck with all the cabins will be in the lower half of the hull, as in any other airship. However, I would change the gondola." Ivy took a clean sheet of paper and started drawing, under Jasper's scrutiny. "I would double the length and add another tier. The entrance and the navigation cabin would be at the first level, while the upper level would have a parlour and an open viewing deck."

"It would look impressive, but that means changing the engines and the navigation cabin," Jasper said.

She didn't intend to give up. Not if she wished to leave her mark on the classic design used in her parents' plans. Besides, it was about time he acknowledged her skill. He would see she was not just a poor aeronaut living off infrequent jobs from the Airharbour Assignments Office.

Ivy was still sorting out her feelings, unable to understand what Jasper meant to her. Since the night they fixed *The Skycradle* together, he had become a reassuring presence, someone whom she needed around. She wasn't sure whether that was friendship – which was only an abstract concept to her.

That morning he looked worn and troubled, and she guessed the reason ought to be the gondotram accident. Ivy had avoided that place. Since her parents' death, she had kept away from such suffering, which she couldn't bear seeing.

"No matter how light our lifting gas is, static lift and two engines will not be enough. Such a craft would still require an enormous amount of effort to get airborne," Jasper said, bringing her back to the reality of his workshop. "A two-tiered double length gondola, and an envelope almost twice as big as a usual one – this is something unheard of."

"What do we need to make it possible?"

Jasper sat on the bench next to her, staring at her sketches.

"We must add at least another pair of engine pods here." He put his finger on the drawing, on the lower half of the envelope. "Leave that to me. I think I can change the engine configuration and redesign the navigation cabin to make it work."

"One more thing." Ivy turned to him, with pleading eyes. "May I choose the colours for this airship?"

"Of course." He was equally surprised and amused. "Choose whatever colours you like."

"My parents used to say that the colours are a mirror of the airship. They chose red for *The Skycradle* because it was the colour of the sunrise. I want blue and gold for our airship, as they are the colours of the sky and the sun at the brightest time of the day."

His smile warmed her heart. She had been afraid he would consider her naïve, or plain stupid, yet his bright blue eyes said otherwise.

"I like your ideas and your stories," he said. "And I do

believe you would make an excellent engineer. Now we only have to find a name for her."

She took a few moments to imagine all the travels their airship would make, all the skies she would cross, how she would shine under the brilliant light of the sun – a royal beauty, elegant in gold and blue.

"*The Cerulean Lady*," Ivy said, returning his smile.

~

"Come in!" Lady Hollingsworth answered the knock at her chamber's door with a trembling voice, making Ivy wonder about her mood to receive guests.

Yet, for the first time since her parents' death, she cared about other people enough to involve herself in their problems.

Rowena was standing in front of the tall windows, her figure a dark outline against the late afternoon mild sun making its way through the half-pulled curtains. She looked unwell and tired, not in the least like a lady eager to attend a ball in the evening.

"I – I just wanted to see how you were faring –" Ivy was clumsy and hesitant. "I heard you were out for most of the day and haven't eaten anything. Are you all right? Shouldn't you prepare for the ball?"

"Oh, Ivy! How can I possibly attend a ball! My heart shatters whenever I think of the unfortunate people in that gondotram. Their suffering, their cries – I cannot forget them!"

"You offered whatever help you could." Ivy admired her, how she always put the others above herself, regardless of their social standing. "I doubt there is another aristocrat as generous and considerate with the less fortunate."

Rowena leaned her forehead on the window, her eyes locked on the garden outside.

"I am not the saint everyone believes," she said. "It is neither generosity nor thoughtfulness. It is guilt. What I am doing for those people is to appease this guilt, to reward them for what they did for someone precious to me. In time, I came to love them, but that does not change my reasons.

"Jasper's twin, who died on *The Golden Griffin*, was my closest friend. We grew up together, and I loved him dearly. I saw in him the older brother I never had."

Rowena kept talking, without looking at her guest. Ivy understood she had opened the door to one of the darkest corners of her soul, and couldn't decide whether to feel honoured or burdened.

"Jasper switched places with him on *The Golden Griffin*, for Jade to earn a promotion in Her Majesty's service after a successful test flight. Given the strict number of crew members, it was not possible for both of them to be on board. Jade received the assignment as a safety officer, while Jasper had to observe the ship from the berth instead of flying with the crew. But that day – the last day Jade was alive – I never thought about him, I never supported him. I spent it with his brother, my heart oblivious of everything else but Jasper. That night I lost them both. Jade died, and Jasper relinquished his soul.

"Losing his twin brother under his very eyes destroyed Jasper. He still blames himself for convincing Jade to take his place. He abandoned his workbench and started drinking in the gin bars of St. Giles. I couldn't bear seeing him waste himself, so I kept chasing him, no matter how afraid I was of that infamous rookery.

"With all the Reform's changes, I was still scared to death each time I went there, wondering whether I would return alive. But the compass clock he made for Seven Dials gave me strength. *To help the lost ones find their way*, he said. I had to help him find his way. The thought of losing him for good frightened me more than that place. I brought him back with those people's help, so I offered them something in return. But not even a thousand charities will ever be able to erase my guilt."

Ivy stood beside her in silent understanding, aware of what Rowena Hollingsworth and Jasper Kendall Asher meant to each other, bound in suffering and guilt. Her soul ached for them, the two people who were the first friends she'd ever had.

~

JASPER FELT a surge of relief when the two mechanical horses halted in front of the Duke of Litchborough's house in Belgrave Square. While riding in the Earl of Wyverstone's carriage from Grosvenor Crescent to their host's mansion, he remembered the hassle of having a decent conversation with Emmeline.

His brother had been of no help either, preferring to ignore them both the entire time.

Edmund helped his wife off the vehicle, and Jasper followed. Steammotors, mechanical horses, and carriages filled the square. Which meant they were among the last ones to arrive.

"'ey guvs! Won't you 'ave a dime to spare for dis poor lad? I'm 'ungry, ain't 'ad a bite all day."

Three pairs of eyes turned in the direction of the voice. In the warm yellow glow of the streetlamps, it took a few moments even for Jasper to recognise Carmina Harcourt in the tattered street urchin with a dirty face who had approached them. Barefoot, wearing a ragged soiled shirt and knee-long breeches kept in place with suspenders, and with her hair carefully hidden under a wig, no one could take her for anything else than a ragamuffin.

"This is preposterous! Such a dirty little rat dares to beg in Belgravia!" Emmeline's sharp voice had nothing but hate and contempt. "Oh, Edmund dearest, let us go in. Such an awful sight makes me unwell. I shall ask someone to send the vermin away."

Edmund shook her off when she started to take his arm. His gaze lingered on the small slender figure who was staring at them with emerald green eyes, and Jasper understood he had recognised her. He also knew that the look his brother exchanged with her meant something. It was not the first time they put a plan in motion in the fleeting second of a glance.

"Perhaps you should take some charity lessons from Lady Hollingsworth." Edmund turned to his wife, this time offering his arm. "You could be more understanding. That boy only wanted to eat, let him be."

Behind them, Jasper tossed a coin, which Carmina caught expertly. For the first time since Jade's death, all three of them were in the same place again, working together.

And it felt like coming home.

"THE ENGINEERS HAVE YET to invent a contraption more wonderful than the musiker." Lady McQuillian was changing the code of the narrow copper cylinders in sheer delight, choosing the next set of waltzes for after the break. "We should be grateful to have such an extraordinary device in our time."

"With all due respect, I believe this brass box is as soulless as a stone. It will never replace a real orchestra. For this reason, I do not own a music maker, and I shall not change that."

"Oh, my dear Herdforthbridge, no musiker will ever compare to your piano. But since you are such a rare treat, we must make do with this otherwise brilliant invention. It's a proof of how our society has evolved."

"I would say our society is rather going astray at an alarming rate," the duke countered. "Look at all these young ladies in our milieu doing whatever they please, going wherever they please. Ten years ago, such behaviour would have been unacceptable."

"A bit of freedom does no harm, and an intelligent lady can tell right from wrong. You are so young, yet so conservative! I am much older, but my heart enjoys all the benefits of this era of novelty."

"Lady McQuillian, you are right," Jasper said. "Our world is constantly moving towards greater things. The musiker brings a new value. Now you can listen to the music you love regardless of the moment or the occasion, without the need to hire an orchestra."

"Perhaps I should play tonight, if only to remind you of the difference between a soul and a machine," the duke said, ignoring Jasper. "If such an interruption is not an inconvenience for the guests, of course."

"Inconvenience? You playing for us would be the most delightful surprise of the evening!"

Jasper raised an eyebrow. Herdforthbridge's unmatched talent with the piano – which he seldom displayed in public – was legendary in London. His unexpected proposal was the chance he sought. Now he could get out of there unnoticed and search Leythfordham's private study. The duke had just offered him the perfect escape.

He disappeared in the crowd with the intention of leaving the ballroom, only to stop when he heard his brother's voice.

"You will find a poor lad outside in the square. Bring him to the kitchens and feed him well. Of course, you must keep an eye on him and see him out."

"Edmund!" Emmeline's high-pitched voice was shaking with anger. "This is outrageous! How can you bring that dirty beggar in here! In the Duke of Litchborough's house, no less!"

"On such a joyous occasion, a bit of generosity is most welcome. I am certain His Grace would agree."

Jasper got close enough to see the recipient of Edmund's orders. Dressed in the uniform of Litchborough household's servants, with her hair properly combed and with no makeup, Hazel was as unrecognisable as her madame. He grinned, finally understanding. Indeed, Edmund and Carmina were very much alike. They came up with the same strategies.

Now they had the perfect excuse to bring her into the house, and it only took a glance for that.

THE PART JASPER hated the most was not knowing what he was searching for. Leaving the ballroom without attracting too much attention had been the most manageable part. Now he had to get to Leythfordham's private study.

He reached the main staircase, keeping away from curious eyes, creeping along the walls, and hiding behind massive pieces of furniture. The murky electric light helped him, making him almost unnoticeable among the surrounding shadows, far from the eyes of the servants who were rushing in and out of the dining room.

Sheltered by the shadows, he found the room he was looking for at the far end of the hallway. Inside, the dim light of a lamp was enough for him to see around.

He stood motionless for a few moments in the middle of the room, his eyes alert and searching his surroundings.

If Leythfordham had anything to hide, it wouldn't be in plain sight.

Think, Jasper Asher. Use your bloody brain!

Nothing caught his attention in the cabinets or behind the books on the shelves. The desk was clear, save for one blank sheet of paper. When he got closer, he realised it was no ordinary stationery.

"Tracing paper! Now let us see if there is anything to trace on it."

In a drawer, Jasper found a small bottle filled with transparent liquid. He poured a drop on the paper and waited. A few moments later, the stain turned from translucent to yellow, revealing the fine lines of what seemed a part of a larger drawing.

"It *was* in plain sight, after all!" Jasper laughed and rolled the document as quickly as he could, replacing it with an ordinary sheet of paper from inside the desk.

Three light taps at the door, which he was already expecting, brought Carmina into the room. She had changed her tattered outfit with the household's maid uniform, from where she took out a folded map.

"You found it? The sewerage system map?"

Carmina's eyes sparkled with excitement. "Of course. In the duke's private library. How about you? What is that scroll?"

"Might be something significant or nothing. I need to spill

some tracing liquid on it to see, but I'm afraid I cannot do that right now. I ought to return downstairs unless I want to draw suspicion upon myself. People are surprised I even made an appearance tonight."

"Then come to the Dove after the ball. Our work here is done. I should go as well, before I get Hazel or anyone else into trouble."

The sudden knock at the door stopped him from asking her if anyone else was another name for Edmund. He pulled her behind a cabinet just when the door was opening.

"Thank heavens everyone is too busy dancing! Care to explain what in the holy name of Christ are you doing?!"

Hearing Emmeline's angry voice, Jasper almost forgot how to breathe, trying to figure out who was the person she was talking to.

"Your Ladyship, I apologise, but this is a serious matter. Otherwise, I would have never left the colliery unattended. Something happened. Some deeds in your name have disappeared."

"What?" Emmeline broke the silence that sank into the room for a few moments. "I surely misunderstood. You couldn't have possibly said you *lost* some of those *transactional documents* with *my name* on them!"

"And that ain't even the worst of it. A few of them were from three years ago."

Shane Gilford. Jasper had the answer. Emmeline's unexpected guest was Shane Gilford, the owner of the Glenbuck colliery.

"Gilford, I swear on God I shall skin you alive, you miserable rat! Why did you keep those documents when I clearly told you to destroy them right after you receive the payment? Is this how you kept your part of the deal?

"But of course, blackmail!" she answered when Gilford

said nothing. "The likes of you are such a disgusting lot! You are lucky I still need you. I shall take care of your mess and find the papers. Meanwhile, you will deliver the mine gas as usual."

"I'm afraid I can't do that. Please forgive me, but I can't send you mine gas until we find the deeds. I can't risk seeing my colliery shut down for illegal activities!"

"I am not paying you a cartload of money to care what you risk! We are too close to give up now. If that stupid of a daughter didn't play hide-and-seek with her parents' research, we would already have that formula. But we shall find it soon. My patience is running thin."

"Pardon me, my lady, but what about me? If the Inspectorates find out, they will send the constabulary, and I am as good as dead. I'm afraid to send mine gas with those trade papers out there, God knows in whose hands!"

Through the crack between the cabinets that hid them, Jasper saw Emmeline's slender hand reaching to Gilford. She was holding a thick ring which he couldn't recognise in the dim light and from that distance.

"Take this," she said. "If anything happens, use it."

"What is this? How can a mere ring protect me?"

"Never look for me again in London. My husband is the last person I want to find out about my connection to Glenbuck. Now leave! This *mere ring* puts you under the protection of the most powerful guild in England. This is the seal of the Engineers Order."

Jasper was grateful for the darkness that hid his astonishment. Emmeline's possible involvement in the gas mine deliveries was not a surprise. Yet her direct connection to the Engineers Order, and even worse, to *The Golden Griffin*, was a completely different matter.

Undoubtedly, it was the same ring Edmund had found

under her carriage. She could only have it from Leythfordham, who was dragging the Order in his affairs. That was almost equal to treason.

"That man must be the owner of the colliery in Glenbuck," Carmina said. With Emmeline and Shane Gilford gone, they came out of their hiding place, not sure what to make of what they had just heard. "If he came here and his papers are missing, it only means one thing. Ginger is back from Scotland – and she is not empty-handed."

~

"WHAT YOU DID tonight was utterly reckless, but I gather you know that. If someone discovered you, both you and Jasper could have been in danger."

The small cloaked figure froze on the wet cobbled street, without turning to where the voice came from.

"But no one did. Edmund, I *know* how to do my work, and you are *perfectly aware* of that," Carmina replied. "Otherwise, you wouldn't have helped me tonight. I would never put Jasper in danger, and he had other things to search for. Finding the map was my duty."

"Hazel could have performed that duty in your stead. You shouldn't have exposed yourself in a place where at least one person could have recognised you! I helped you because you left me with no choice! And bloody hell, Carmina, look at me! I want to see your face when I am talking to you!"

"We are able to hear each other, and that should be enough. You are right, I shall revise my conduct in this investigation. Now I request permission to leave."

"Which I am not granting you," Edmund said, stepping out from the blind spot that hid him. "You haven't changed at all, always acting as you see fit and ignoring the approved plan of a mission. Your recklessness still infuriates the hell out of me, regardless of how brilliant you are. But, damnation! I have missed you every single day of the last three years! If you didn't want to see me, you should have stayed away from me tonight. Do not appear before my eyes in whatever disguise and expect me to let you go, because I shall not."

He reached for her hand and turned her to him, his eyes locked on hers. The next thing he knew he was kissing her like a madman, his mind empty of any other thought, his three years resolve to keep his distance shattered in an instant.

She clutched his waistcoat, only to push him away as hard as she could.

"Edmund, rest assured. Both Jasper and the investigation are safe with me. There was no need for you to lurk in the rain near the servants' entrance to explain what I must or must not do. Return to the life you have chosen. I bear no grudges against you. Though late, I understood your other reason for what you did three years ago – Herdforthbridge is fortunate to have you as a friend. Your marriage turned the attention from the brother's scandal to the sister. But no matter how noble your reasons, they change nothing. Don't you dare meddle into my life again!"

She vanished into the darkness before he could reply.

Return to the life you have chosen.

Carmina's words were still resonating in his mind a few hours later, over the dull sound of the carriage's wheels.

On the bench in front of him, Emmeline was silent, focused on the scenery reeling before her eyes on the other side of the window. She was beautiful, one of the most admired women in London, and the image of the perfect wife.

Yet, to him, she only was the reflection of his own failure, compromise, and defeat.

"What were you doing upstairs in Leythfordham's mansion? To my knowledge, the ball did not extend beyond the ground floor."

The sudden question startled Emmeline enough to make her look at him.

"That is unexpected," she said, with a visible trace of sarcasm in her voice. "Edmund Asher, the Earl of Wyverstone, caring enough as to spy on his wife."

"If I spied on you, I would have already had my answer. I only happened to see you coming down the staircase."

"Worry not, Edmund dearest, I was not having a tryst under your nose – if that was what you were suggesting. I was only resting for a bit in the library in Lady McQuillian's company, as I was feeling unwell."

"Why are you like this each time I try to reach out to you? Emmeline, I am not your enemy. I am your husband. Your arrogance does not make things any better."

"I am like what?" she asked, her glance focused again on the carriage window. "Need I remind you that I am not the one who has first forgotten you are my husband?"

Again, that insinuation she always refused to explain. Her mockery irked him, but he was not in the mood to continue a conversation that would have led nowhere.

He had long since abandoned his attempt to understand her. His wife's sudden, unexplainable change after *The Golden Griffin* had estranged him even more from her, denying him any possibility to obtain the information he needed.

~

Later that night, alone in his private study, Edmund took an old letter out of a cabinet. Though faded, he could still read the handwriting on the yellow paper.

> *My man in Glenbuck confirmed the Blackwells' return for The Golden Griffin's test flight the following week. Her Majesty's office chose the crew.*
>
> *The Engineers Order has no say in the matter, so insisting would be useless. However, Jasper's engine pods might be useful for your endeavour. Perhaps you will show everyone he is but a presumptuous boy, unfit for such a position.*
>
> *If everything goes as planned during the test, the Queen will need to postpone or even cancel The Golden Griffin's official maiden flight – to the amusement of the entire beau monde.*
>
> *For the Royal House, such a blow will be hard to take.*

He folded the paper again, looking instinctively towards the door. The same door Oscar Bashford, the Duke of Herdforthbridge, had opened years ago to bring him that letter, one week after the damned airship accident.

"I accept your offer," he had said, with no other introduction. "I shall be your shadow whenever you need me. Working for you until the end of my days will not suffice to atone for what I did."

Edmund raised an eyebrow, trying to find a logical explanation behind the duke's words. For two years, he had been constantly rejecting his offer to work for him officially. Why had he suddenly decided otherwise?

"Oscar, are you drunk? Whatever happened to you?"

The duke handed him a crumpled piece of paper. "I did something terrible. I shall not ask for your forgiveness, for I do not deserve it. But at least let me repay my debt in any way I can.

"Like you, I did not trust Emmeline's connections with the Engineers Order, and her friendship with Leythfordham," he said, while Edmund read the document, his eyes darkening. "So, I had my people tail her. Especially when she kept visiting our home suspiciously often after she married you. I discovered she came there to send letters. One night, my men retrieved the letter you have in your hands. Of course, according to the general opinion, a gang of blokes attacked her servant to rob her. This was shortly before *The Golden Griffin* accident."

"Why are you telling me this only now? Who was this letter addressed to? What does it even mean?"

"I believed someone was using my sister, but I never found out who, no matter how hard I tried. When no other information surfaced, I wanted at least to stop a possible disaster. Given Leythfordham's influence, I asked him to do something to prevent that flight. I was an imbecile. I destroyed lives trying to protect my foolish sister. And betrayed my best friend, who went as far as to relinquish his happiness to smother the scandal in which that awful woman dragged me when she fled to Australia, leaving me like a fool. Do not think I haven't realised why you wanted to marry Emmeline so hurriedly."

In the silence that followed, Edmund opened the glass door of his cabinet for a decanter and two glasses. He had never seen the duke in such a state. His eyes were hollow. Fatigue and guilt had turned his fine features into a harrowing picture.

"I am taking up on your offer, but you have nothing to atone for. I accept because I need someone like you to work with me," he said at last, handing him the glass of brandy. "You are not guilty of anything. My decisions are my own and I shall not discuss them any further. Now I am absolutely certain you are not a traitor. *That ship must not fly*. Carmina heard you at Claridge's. She believed you were plotting something, but I trusted you. You did not betray me. On the contrary."

"But you lost so much because of my selfishness! I agreed with you marrying my sister although you loved another woman – for I knew Emmeline wanted you as her husband since she was a girl. I did not tell you about the letter because I was scared of what could happen to her. She is so spoilt, and always ends up in trouble. I would never trust anyone to take care of her as I trust you. She might not be the most tolerable person, but at least try to understand her. I doubt she knew about that tragedy before it occurred."

Edmund gazed at the glass wall mounted in wrought iron frames, his back at Herdforthbridge. "I lost so much because of those who rigged *The Golden Griffin*, not you. Oscar, you are a man of honour who would never betray his principles. You could have destroyed this letter. Yet here you are, burdened with guilt. Worry not. I promise I shall try to understand Emmeline."

And he had tried to keep the promise made that night to the Duke of Herdforthbridge. To his only real friend.

That was the life he had chosen. A long struggle to figure out whether the woman to whom he had given his name out of compromise was a mere tool in someone else's game, or the most dangerous person he had ever encountered.

LONG PAST MIDNIGHT, Jasper and Carmina were standing near the small table in Carmina's study at the Cinnamon Dove. The paper Jasper had found on the Marquess of Leythfordham's desk was soaked in tracing liquid, which had started to change colour. It was turning yellow, revealing the drawing hidden under the first layer.

"A map." Jasper stared at the intricate lines. "Why would you want to hide a map with tracing paper?"

"This map has something familiar. Look at this one." Carmina unfolded the sewerage system map she had stolen. "It seems the same place, yet somehow different."

"It *is* the same place!" Jasper said, leaning over the maps. "The only difference is that the map on the tracing paper is one level lower in the underground. If my gut feeling is right, your map is only a cover for what lies underneath it."

"I can't understand these markings in red. They don't look like sewage tunnels, but rather like some sort of rooms. Also, nothing here resembles an entrance. It is the only thing missing from the hidden map. We could try using the access holes on the map I found, but I doubt they are the same."

"We shall find out soon. Now I am more curious to see the papers Ginger brought from Scotland."

Carmina took out a leather binder from her drawer and handed it to Jasper. He opened it greedily, as if it contained all the answers to the questions that had been haunting him for three years, to all his nightmares and deepest despair.

They remained silent for a few moments. Suddenly, the room seemed too small, the rug too thick, the light too bright, while Jasper read everything for the second time, to make sure he hadn't misunderstood.

"I'll kill her!" he growled, throwing the binder on the table. "If she is responsible for what happened three years ago, I swear I'll kill her with my own hands!"

The first document in the open binder was staring at him in silent mockery. It was a deed in Emmeline's name, dated Friday, 27th of May 1892 – during her visit with Edmund at the Blackwells' cottage in Glenbuck, two weeks before *The Golden Griffin* exploded.

"Charcoal, saltpetre, sulphur. Delivery address to be communicated at a later time –" Jasper read aloud, tracing each line with his finger, his blue eyes darkening. "Order signed by Lady Emmeline Asher, Countess of Wyverstone.

"If you combine those things, you only get one result." He clasped the wooden frame of the armchair next to him so hard that his knuckles turned white. "And that is gunpowder."

13

Jasper cleared his throat, trying to silence the murmur of the other members of the Engineers Order who were still finding their seats on the wooden benches. Benedict Quimby was presiding over the assembly from his high stand in front of the amphitheatre. Theophilus Hollingsworth, honorary president and royal mechanic, was sitting next to him, as Her Majesty's delegate.

"Honourable gentlemen, as the technical investigator of the gondotram incident, I shall present my findings." Jasper's voice sounded calm and steady, in complete contradiction to how he felt after a sleepless night and a thousand ways he imagined himself killing Emmeline Rexworth Asher. "I was certain the wagon was rigged, for we all know its propelling system is flawless. However, the only explanation I could find was a faulty gripping mechanism. This matter falls entirely within the Engineers Order's authority – and not the constabulary's. No investigation is necessary."

Play stupid if need be. He had no other choice but to follow Edmund's advice, as risky as it was to lie in an Engineers Order's assembly. But he couldn't tell them the truth. He needed to find out who was responsible for all the mess without any meddling from the constabulary.

"If I may!" The Marquess of Leythfordham pulled the knob that triggered the small copper ring bell in front of him.

Benedict Quimby raised his hand, allowing him to speak.

"Of course, we were aware of what Jasper Asher explained. However, we must think about what caused such tragedy. The Inspectorates found no culprit because there is none. The only finding of a sound scientific reasoning would be an unusual and intense circulation of powerful earthquake waves, which are too dangerous for the Londoners who are dwelling there."

"A very rational conclusion," Jasper said. "However, the danger is rather exaggerated. I doubt we shall witness such strange geological occurrences too often, so we have no reason to worry about the Londoners in St. Giles."

Playing stupid was becoming quite a burdensome endeavour.

"But, of course, we have!" the marquess countered. "Think about those who died in that fated gondotram. Or about those who might have died in Lady Hollingsworth's school! We cannot put those people in peril any longer. We must evacuate the area!"

Playing stupid be damned. At least I tried.

"Everyone here is acquainted with your plans to turn the former rookery in St. Giles into your private airharbour. No decent member of this Order would support that idea. Taking advantage of such an unfortunate event is nefarious and by no means appropriate."

Jasper's bold words stirred the murmurs anew. Slandering another member of the Order was unheard of – and hardly tolerated.

"Oh, and who is accusing me of such unworthy

behaviour, when my intentions are in that poor community's best interests? One with no activity and no contribution to this esteemed Order in the past three years? Who forgot the etiquette of our guild and uses his brother's power to keep himself in the good graces of Her Majesty?"

"Enough!" To everyone's surprise, Theophilus Hollingsworth's gavel struck the wooden surface of his lectern. He rarely used his honorary president status, but when he did, no one disputed his authority, as he was there on behalf of the Royal House. "Gentlemen, I must demand that you keep such petty quarrels and accusations away from this place. I shall also remind you the reason we are here today. Which is to discuss possible measures to avoid other similar incidents."

His master wanted to protect him. Jasper felt equally ashamed and furious. He was well aware that the Marquess of Leythfordham was talking the other members into excluding him from the Engineers Order. Jasper was not allowed to take even one wrong step until he completed Her Majesty's airship. An open argument in the assembly could be the spark to banish him. Yet he couldn't stand still. Much as he respected Theophilus Hollingsworth, he couldn't let Leythfordham have his way.

"Master Hollingsworth is right," Senior Lord Benedict Quimby interfered. "However, I would like to hear the Marquess of Leythfordham's point without further interruptions. Please, do go on."

"The only measure we can take is to clear the entire area," the marquess replied before Jasper could say anything else. "I'm afraid Lady Hollingsworth's idea of reopening the school is inconsiderate and hazardous. What if another incident happens again? Would she take responsibility for a tragedy that could occur there? This charity game of hers must end at once! The gin bars and all the other establishments must close, and the inhabitants should relocate to safer neighbourhoods. We should redesign the entire place. It will involve an enormous amount of work, but it is for the greater good of the community."

"And how exactly do you want it redesigned?" Jasper asked. "By turning it into an airharbour? After getting rid of everything and everyone who might go against you? Her Majesty granted Lady Hollingsworth the right to open a new school. Now it has become a hospital for the people wounded in the gondotram accident. What will you do? Throw them in the street and bring down the building?"

"Mind your words, Jasper! Else I shall be obliged to call off this assembly!" Theophilus Hollingsworth tried to temper him, but it was too late. Jasper had said enough to attract the hostility of at least half of the Engineers Order.

"I demand the members' vote!" the marquess said, without even glancing at the honorary president. "I demand that the Order decides upon my proposal!"

"I thought of something that might fit this situation." Benedict Quimby beckoned him to take his seat. "As we all know, with our help, the Architects Order is working on a new dwelling prototype which they will implement in the industrial districts at the outskirts of London. Houses raised on platforms that can change their position through a cogwheel system powered by steam engines. Moving the residents of that neighbourhood into these houses would be an excellent occasion to test this novelty. They would benefit from the latest inventions of our Orders, and we can clear and redesign the area for better purposes. Gentlemen, do you agree?"

To Jasper's horror, all the members raised their hands. They all thought they were witnessing innovation. Benedict

Quimby believed he was doing something good for those people, but the only purpose of the evacuation was to help Leythfordham. Jasper had thought he could protect them, protect Rowena and her school, but he felt powerless and defeated. The only way to save them was to discover what was hidden underneath St. Giles – and he was running out of time.

~

JASPER LEFT THE ASSEMBLY HALL, his head spinning. He went up to the second floor, to the secluded recess that hosted Edmund's office in the Classified Affairs wing. The soft light of the noon crept inside the building through the tall windows of the corridor facing the interior gardens. In the distance, the rumbling water of the mechanical waterfall was thundering off its giant cogwheel into the narrow space below it, only to be driven up again by the continuous movement of the system.

He found his older brother staring out at the waterfall from his office's windows, as he always did when he was deep in thought. The sound of the door opening and closing made him turn, and Jasper handed him the binder where he had all the documents received from Carmina.

"Emmeline could not have done this alone," Edmund concluded after reading Jasper's papers. "She is neither intelligent enough nor has the resources to conspire anything on the scale of blasting the royal airship on her own. She is covering for someone. What bothers me is that I cannot fathom her reasons."

"You realise what these papers mean, yet you don't seem surprised your wife's name is on them."

"I found it weird when she insisted on accompanying me

in the middle of nowhere when I visited the Blackwells in Glenbuck. She asked me to allow her to stroll around while I was working. That was no place for sightseeing, so it made me wonder. I told you I had my reasons to tail her."

Jasper's eyes flickered with a new realisation. "It was *her*, and not the duke whom you suspected from the very beginning! I wonder what else you are still keeping from me. Is it entertaining to see me discovering things you already knew? Such as confirming for you that your beloved wife is a blasted murderer?!"

"Bloody hell, Jasper! I knew nothing of this! Do you think I would sink so low as to share the house – *our home* – with the woman who *killed* our brother!? Who the hell do you take me for? I was certain she was involved, but I thought she didn't know what she was doing. I thought someone was using her. But I agree. Nobody purchases saltpetre, charcoal, and sulphur without knowing what they are doing. I never realised she could be part of a damned plot on her own will. Had I known – Had I found out in time – Jade would be still alive, and I would have never –"

Edmund stopped abruptly, and Jasper could do nothing but stare. It was one of the moments he wished to understand his brother, to be able to reach out to him.

"She will suffer the consequences, regardless of her reasons." Edmund took a deep breath to steady his voice. "We lost too much – *I* lost too much because of her and those in her league. I swear on all I hold dear that this time they will all go down with her."

~

IVY GOT off the Hollingsworth family carriage in front of Jasper's workshop on Tallis Street, like she had every day for the past several weeks. But that time was different. She waited until the coachman was out of sight, then took out the key she had stolen from Eudora Carraway.

She didn't like it at all, but it was a necessary intrusion. Jasper had gone to the Inspectorates for the Engineers Order meeting and hadn't called her that day at the workshop. She was lucky her nursemaid worked for him and had that weird and complicated key which allowed her to enter. Now she had enough time to sniff around, perhaps find an answer or two.

I'm sorry, Jasper Asher, but I need to find out what you are hiding from me. If I am in such danger that I need to be kept away from my own house and escorted as if I were the queen of England, then it would be only fair to know the reason.

It was not that she hated the Hollingsworth mansion. Ivy liked the place, as she liked Rowena and her father. They were kind to her, but she still missed her home. With all the freedom to move around taken away from her, she felt caged.

She longed for *The Skycradle*, the airharbour, the view of the airships docked in their berths. She didn't like being guarded – it was a strange feeling. The sooner she found out what it was all about, the better – and Jasper ought to have the answer to that annoying riddle.

She found nothing.

"Of course, he must have some blasted contraptions to hide his important stuff!" Ivy let out a frustrated sigh. She went upstairs and opened the door to the only room left unexplored.

Jasper's bedchamber was surprisingly stark, not at all what she had expected from a nobleman. But he was different from other aristocrats. She had to give him credit for that. It was awkward and embarrassing to invade his privacy, but it was her only chance to look for clues that might help her understand the danger looming upon her.

A few books, the clothes in the wooden wardrobe, a washbasin, and a copper ewer. A bare plank floor without a carpet. His crumpled nightshirt thrown on the unmade bed.

Even a hermit's room is more lavish than this, she thought as she returned downstairs. Her little trespassing adventure had come to an end without any result. The only thing left for her was to confront him and ask for the truth.

At least she had the day for herself. Rowena was at her school turned into hospital, Master Hollingsworth had his duties to attend at the Engineers Order, and Eudora was out to run errands. None of them were home, and everyone believed she was at the workshop. It was the perfect occasion for a bit of free time alone.

The crude late June sun was gleaming on the red bricks of the warehouses aligned close to Blackfriars Bridge. The docks and the skystation were livelier than ever, with people rushing in and out, shouting or just minding their own business. The skystation lift was creeping on the wall like a huge metal spider, carrying its load to the platforms. Terrifying as it was, the gruesome accident still couldn't keep people away from the gondotram. She felt the urge to run up the massive stairs up to Platform 7, go to the airharbour, and fly *The Skycradle*.

Ivy was still pondering whether to pursue that idea, go to her old house in Clerkenwell or return to the Hollingsworth mansion before anyone found out what she had done, when a carriage stopped next to her.

It couldn't be an ordinary coach, Ivy decided after a first glance. Its ironwork was exquisite, and the two mechanical horses had the latest wire-cogwheel systems. She looked at the wrought iron patterns that covered the vehicle, only to discover the Earl of Wyverstone's family crest.

"Rats and caterpillars!" Ivy grumbled in sheer annoyance. "Can't you lot just let me be at least for one blasted day? Why is that frightening man after me?"

But it was not Edmund Asher who got off the carriage. The coachman opened the door, helping out a petite woman with blonde curls and thin lips. She was wearing a green dress of the latest fashion, which complemented her pale blue eyes. The woman was beautiful and elegant, one of those refined high society ladies. Yet her cold smile unnerved Ivy.

"Good day, Miss Blackwell. I was looking for Jasper but saw you leaving his workshop. Since he was not there, I could only assume you had a key – which is extraordinary, given the strict rules he has for that place. Am I right?"

No, you are not.

Ivy cursed her incurable habit of acting on impulse, which had made her take the bloody key from Eudora.

"I do not recall us ever having met."

"Oh, pardon my rudeness. I am Emmeline Rexworth Asher, Countess of Wyverstone. Jasper's sister-in-law. He speaks of you so often, so it felt like I already knew you and forgot the basic courtesy of introducing myself."

That was strange. Ivy knew Jasper well enough to be sure he did not speak of her. Or at least not as often as that woman suggested.

"It is lovely to meet you in person, so please allow me to offer you a ride in my carriage. I would be delighted to accompany you to Lady Hollingsworth's house. If that is where you are going, of course."

By their society's standards, refusing her was rude, so she had no choice but to accept. Lady Emmeline Asher was

Jasper's family, so at least she was safe. And she had to make sure the woman wasn't taking her for a thief. The last thing Ivy wanted was for Jasper to find out she had searched his house in his absence.

"You are very kind," Ivy said with a tentative smile. "That would be most appreciated."

She followed the countess into the carriage, which was much smaller on the inside than it looked on the outside. All the curtains were pulled, but the darkness was rather pleasant.

"You were right. I was going to Lady Hollingsworth's mansion." She couldn't reveal her other plans for the day.

"Of course. I am happy Rowena found a friend. She was such a solitary girl, hardly tolerating anyone but Jade Asher around her."

"She is considerate and kind, and must have had her reasons. I don't like talking about others when they are not present."

"Then you would rather sneak into their house? Miss Blackwell, I wonder what you were looking for. Don't try to fool me. I know Jasper didn't give you the key. I am *extremely* curious to find out what he is hiding from you. It must be important to make you trespass."

Her harsh voice startled Ivy, who decided she didn't like Emmeline Rexworth Asher. The carriage felt stuffy and confining, and she only wanted to get off and run as fast as she could.

"I think I'll walk. Pardon me, but I don't feel too well. I need some fresh air."

"Oh, I'm afraid that is not possible. There are still many questions you need to answer, and I had quite enough of your hide-and-seek game. You are coming with me."

Ivy could only see a hand reaching out of the small

window behind her, covering her nose and mouth with a blue napkin, before the stingy odour on it made her too drowsy to keep her eyes open.

"Put her in the back and keep an eye on her." Lady Asher's voice seemed blurred and distant, as if she was speaking from a thousand miles away. "We shall take care of her later."

At last, clasping her fingers around the pocket where she had Jasper's key, Ivy drifted into sleep.

~

JASPER GOT BACK to his workshop just past noon. The commotion at the Engineers Order assembly and his meeting with Edmund were enough to give him a terrible headache, especially after the events of the previous night. He needed to clear his mind, and he was happy Ivy wasn't there. Much as he loved working on *The Cerulean Lady*, that day he couldn't focus on anything. It was too early for a drink at the Copper Kettle, so he went upstairs to sleep.

But sleep refused to come. One hour later he was still awake, staring at the ceiling, his thoughts a relentless whirlwind of anger, frustration, and disappointment.

A walk to the Hollingsworth mansion would help him cool his head. He also owed an apology to his master, who had shielded him at the assembly earlier. He had let his temper get the better of him when he could lose everything. Though he didn't fancy becoming Theophilus Hollingsworth's successor, he knew how much his master wanted that of him. It could also give him the power he needed to protect the people and places he held so dear.

"Master Jasper! Why are you here?" Eudora Carraway was staring at him from the doorstep of the Hollingsworth house's main entrance. In normal circumstances, he would have found her startled face amusing, but her overreaction made him alert.

"Why are you asking me that? Is there a reason I should not be here? May I come in?"

"Oh, pardon me, my lord." The woman bowed, her face red with embarrassment. "I was surprised you left Miss Ivy alone at the workshop. That lass could set it on fire for all I know."

"What?!" Jasper stopped midway in the vestibule, his headache suddenly increasing to an almost unbearable level. "What do you mean I left Ivy at the workshop?"

"Since she was not with you, I supposed she was still working. Has she gone somewhere else, by any chance? The carriage drove her to the workshop in the morning, as usual."

"Is that what she told you? Are you certain? I never saw her today. She had the day off."

"As certain as I am of my own name, my lord. That lass will be the death of me! Why did she lie? Such behaviour would have infuriated her parents!"

"Mrs Carraway, worry not. It's still early. Ivy will be back soon enough. Perhaps she went to the airharbour to check on *The Skycradle*."

He tried to offer reassurance, though a dark, cold foreboding was gripping him. Ivy could be impulsive and hasty, but she was not a liar.

Ivy Blackwell, what the bloody hell are you doing? What games are you playing?

"Just in time for a cup of tea, dear boy! Come, we have plenty to talk about after today's events."

Trying to hide his distress, Jasper followed Theophilus Hollingsworth into his private library. He could only hope he was right, and Ivy would return before dinner.

And she'd better have a bloody good explanation for her stunt.

"My lord, if I may –" Eudora Carraway entered with the tea tray. "Forgive me, but I've noticed something. My workshop key is missing, and the only one who knew about it was Miss Ivy – I don't know what is in that mind of hers, God forbid! To take my key and go out without telling anyone!"

Jasper only spared a moment to apologise to his master before leaving the library in haste. He was paying the price for underestimating Ivy Blackwell and hiding things from her. She must have sneaked into his house to find answers on her own. But he had made sure his place had no answers to offer to anyone, and she should have been back a long time ago. He had to find her before someone else did.

He darted down the stairs, only to come to a halt at the base, his eyes filled with horror. In one instant, he forgot about the morning assembly at the Engineers Order, about his work, even about how Ivy Blackwell had vanished with his key.

Jack Killen was coming in, carrying a limp bundle in his arms.

"Master Jasper, 'er Ladyship was stabbed! We need a doctor while she is still breathing!"

A few moments later, Jasper was rushing back upstairs, clutching Rowena's body covered in blood.

14

Rowena opened her eyes, struggling to distinguish her surroundings in the dim light. Through her blurred vision, in the mellow glow of the candle, she recognised the thick blue curtains of her room. They were covering the tall windows entirely, making it hard to tell whether it was day or night.

A sharp ache stabbed her chest, prompting her to clutch the bedsheets. Warm and drenched in sweat, they emanated a sour odour of illness and medicine.

But, as painful as it was to breathe, as feverish as she felt, she was grateful for being alive.

She vaguely recalled going to her steammotor behind the school building, starting the boiler and waiting. Then, the sudden searing pain as the blade pierced her flesh, the silhouette of an unknown man darkening before her hazy eyes, the voice she didn't recognise.

No hard feelings, lady, but I 'ave plenty o' mouths to feed. Nuffing personal, just so you know –

She only remembered a dirty long-sleeved shirt – which was far from enough.

"You are awake, my child. I never imagined time could pass so slowly. The last hours seemed a lifetime."

"Father –" She tried to sit up, but her body refused to listen. "How did I end up here? I thought –"

"A good man carried you from the school, and Jasper brought your steammotor back. The poor boy looked like he was going to kill someone."

Rowena struggled to speak, her voice still too weak. "Where is Jasper? Is he not here anymore?"

"He left to help Mrs Carraway. Miss Blackwell wished for a bit of adventure and disappeared without telling anyone. Jasper went to search for her."

Rowena frowned. Ivy was not the kind to worry everyone for the sake of adventure. What if she was lying unconscious in some place where nobody could see her, completely helpless, fighting death or even dead? The thought made her blood run cold. She tried to say something, but her throat froze, all strength left her body.

She closed her eyes again, certain that Jasper would find her friend and bring her back.

She will live. However, the wound is deep and too close to her lungs, and it will only worsen in time. I cannot tell if in one year or ten, but she will contract the lung disease. If she is careful, she might live even twenty years from now. But it's a gamble.

The doctor's words were still echoing in Jasper's mind, as he was slowly comprehending their terrible meaning. She was alive, yet he could lose her any time.

"Please, don't tell Master Hollingsworth," he had begged their family doctor. "Rowena wouldn't want him to suffer on her account."

"I'm afraid I cannot do that. If I keep such a secret from a patient's family, the Doctors Order might exclude me. Send me to the gaol even. I must tell both of them the truth."

The sun was still up, yet the Copper Kettle was crowded when Jasper arrived from the airharbour. He wanted to drink to oblivion, to forget about the unfortunate events that had happened in less than a day.

At least Hadrian Hayes from the Airharbour Assignments Office had given him one little reassurance in the overwhelming mess of the day. Ivy hadn't disappeared. She was flying *The Skycradle*. He had felt the urge to wait for her at the airharbour and spit in her face how he hated liars and self-centred people, who did as they pleased while worrying everyone.

In the end, a double gin to cool down his temper had been a better idea than an altercation with Ivy Blackwell.

"Master Jasper, 'ow's 'er Ladyship? Will she be well?"

"Yes, Jack, she will. But her recovery will take a while."

"What about the school? We 'eard those people today saying vey would send the wounded to the 'ospital and close 'er Ladyship's school."

"What people? Lady Hollingsworth's school is granted by Her Majesty. Nobody can close it that easily."

"Some gents from the Inspectorates. Vey came 'ere to sniff around. Didn't look too friendly."

"Did they say what they wanted?" Jasper asked, gulping down his gin.

The new detail only added to his uneasiness.

"Only that the entire area might be cleared soon for an important project. And that vey would send all of us to some weird moving houses at the outskirts. Master Jasper, we don't want to leave our 'omes!"

The Engineers Order. Will they really move these people to the housing project and redesign the rookery? All because of two incidents which are still unresolved?

~

Jasper wiped Rowena's feverish forehead, squeezing the cloth in the washbasin. He felt helpless, raw pain gnawing at his chest. A single blade had taken years off her life. She was alive, yet on the brink of death.

"Don't leave me, Rowe –" he mumbled, caressing her livid cheek. "Don't leave my side too soon. I love you, Rowe. I love you so much –"

He stopped, aware of the words he had uttered. To say them out loud was frightening and incredible and painful and too much to bear. He pressed his lips lightly on her temple, before leaving the room to join Theophilus Hollingsworth in his private library.

"The annual grand assembly is almost upon us," his master said. "If your presentation of the new royal airship is as outstanding as I expect, the members' vote will be but a formality."

"We have completed the airship plans," Jasper said, his thoughts back to *The Cerulean Lady*. "I daresay it will far exceed everyone's expectations."

"I do not doubt that. However, I need to inform you of a rather unpleasant event. The Marquess of Leythfordham came here while you were out."

"His wish to be your successor is not exactly a secret."

"Indeed. However, he asked for Rowena's hand in marriage. It was the second time he came to my house for that reason."

Jasper clenched his fists, his eyes wide with astonishment. "Rowena would never agree!"

"Of course, she would not. But the marquess found out what happened to her. He will protect her if she marries him and I retire to the countryside, naming him as my successor. If I refuse, and she keeps her charity in St. Giles, only God knows what could happen the next time. He wants to turn the place into an airharbour, and Rowena's school is the most important thing standing in his way. Her Majesty's letter of approval is her most powerful shield."

The royal mechanic moved his gaze from his former apprentice to the bookshelves behind his desk before continuing.

"Dear boy, I know you are deeply in love with my daughter. Or, better said, I know you are deeply in love with each other. If you asked for her hand, I would approve without blinking. But I am quite certain you will not do that."

Jasper leaned on the frame of the tall window, his eyes focused on the streetlamp outside. "You are right. I have always loved Rowena. But I have nothing to offer. I do not intend to return to my nobleman status, and I cannot ask her to live with me in a small chamber above a workshop. To relinquish the life to which she is accustomed. Even if she agrees to share her life with me as I am now, I could never accept. She deserves much more than a man like me. But I shall never allow that bloody bastard of Leythfordham blackmail you to have her. Rowena's ordeal comes strangely in handy for his purposes. If he is involved in any way in what happened to her, he will regret the day he was born."

~

"ATTEMPTED MURDER AND THREATENING MASTER HOLLINGSWORTH!" Jasper said, struggling to contain his anger. Much as he wished to go straight to the Inspectorates, he needed to see his brother first. “Moreover, three people whom the marquess sent out to rig Ivy’s airship are now nowhere to be found. If we connect this incident to the other disappearances related to a new factory nobody can locate, we might have a much bigger case. I do not exclude the possibility that all the recent incidents in St. Giles have one common cause. I shall file a request to the constabulary to arrest him.”

“As I recall, you work for the Office of Classified Affairs, and not for the constabulary,” Edmund said. “Leave them out of this. How many times must I tell you to find evidence first before carelessly throwing accusations? What if he is not guilty? You will become the laughingstock of the Inspectorates and attract attention upon yourself. I cannot allow that!”

But Jasper’s opinion differed from Edmund’s, and he intended to hold his ground.

“The constables are already investigating, so why not tell them the truth? I doubt Leythfordham is innocent!”

“I don’t want the constabulary to peek their noses into our business. You will do nothing until I tell you to. Suit yourself, Jasper! Don’t let love blind your judgement! Your feelings are turning you into a liability again!”

“What would *you* know about love and feelings!” Jasper’s words were rolling out like drops of venom. “A man for whom marriage is only a means to solve a case should not talk about love!”

Edmund didn’t answer. He turned his gaze towards the setting sun that flooded his private study in shades of intense red and orange. The windows cased in the tall wrought iron frames were facing the most secluded corner of their home garden, surrounded by a stone fence covered in moss.

“You ought to understand that the slightest mistake can

compromise everything. I believed three years were enough for you to recover from your slumber – I know how good you are. However, I failed to see that your feelings for Lady Hollingsworth might endanger your activity as an agent. If you cannot forget about your private matters while on a mission which we need to carry out in utmost secrecy until we find enough evidence to proceed to further action, I shall remove you from service."

His brother was right. They were so close to revealing a potentially illegal operation, and to finally finding out the truth about *The Golden Griffin*. Edmund could not make any move without solid evidence, and Jasper's duty as an agent was to find whatever evidence his superior needed to send out his men. For that, he had to set his heart aside and use his brain.

The evening was almost reaching its end, with the red hues of the sun fading away into the colder shades of darkness. Ivy should have been home by now, but Edmund's speakerbox was the only way to make sure.

Moments later, Mrs Carraway was lamenting at the other end of the line.

"Master Jasper, thank heavens you asked! With everything that happened to Lady Hollingsworth, I had no one to turn to. Miss Ivy is not here, and I know nothing about her whereabouts. I hoped she was flying her airship and would return for dinner, as you said. But she never came home!"

NOW I'M CERTAIN! Jasper pressed his foot hard on the speed pedal of Edmund's steammotor. *They aren't after the airship plans! They are after the laevium production formula! If they*

abducted Ivy, they must need it badly. At least they won't kill her. They are running out of time, but time for what?

Her words from the night they flew *The Skycradle* together resonated in his mind. *I never ask for help because I have no one to turn to.*

Now she had. Ivy Blackwell had long ceased to be his charge. She was his *friend*. He would find her no matter what and bring her home.

He stopped the vehicle in front of the Airharbour Assignments Office, which he found still open.

Hadrian Hayes was preparing to leave when he entered.

"Your Lordship! How can I help you this time?"

He glanced over his thick spectacles, his eyes round and small like a mole's. Jasper didn't like Hayes, much less trust him.

"When exactly did you see Ivy Blackwell today? I am expecting you to tell the truth."

"There is nothing more to tell. I saw her airship today, late at noon, when she took off from her berth. Then returned before sunset. *The Skycradle* is docked."

"Did you see Ivy with your own eyes?"

"No. But I could never mistake *The Skycradle*. I saw her taking off, then landing back. It was Miss Blackwell's airship."

"Only that she never had Miss Blackwell on board! If she had any commission, you should know. You approve each airship request! Who asked for *The Skycradle* today?"

"Forgive me, but that is a bit of information I am not able to provide. Our clients might want to remain anonymous. I cannot break their trust."

"But I can break your neck." Jasper was breaching the Office of Classified Affairs' code of conduct, which forbade him to use threats on defenceless people and without evidence of involvement into a case. But it was a desperate situation which required drastic measures. He was towering over the airharbour clerk, eyeing him with a menacing look. The man took a few steps behind, cowering in fear. "You either lie and that airship never moved from her berth, or *someone other* than Miss Blackwell flew her. I shall ask once more. *Who* requested *The Skycradle* today?"

"The Inspectorates made the request – the Engineers Order's office. On behalf of the Marquess of Leythfordham."

~

COMPLETE DARKNESS and an almost unbearable stench of rot and mould were the first things Ivy was aware of when she came to her senses. She felt her way around, crawling alongside the wet stone wall until she reached something that might have been a door. As expected, the latch was locked.

It took her only a few steps to cross the tiny enclosure. Small and dark places had always frightened her, and that one seemed the materialisation of her innermost fears – to be all alone, without the slightest idea where she was.

She clasped her throat in a desperate attempt to breathe.

Escaping looked like an impossible undertaking. But she could at least make her presence known to whoever had brought her there. Survival came first, even though it meant meeting her abductors.

Gathering all her strength and trying to control her searing fear, she started pounding on the door, screaming her lungs out.

"Open this blasted door! Open it! What the hell is this place! Open the damned door!"

She kept shouting and hitting until she heard the hollow echo of boots on stone, followed by the light of a torch coming her way. When the key turned into the hole, the yellow glow revealed her surroundings, along with a middle-aged man wearing a leather mask.

Ivy could only see his eyes and half of his face, which she didn't recognise.

She looked around – high stone walls, the rusted iron door, and a hard floor with nothing on it.

"Rats and caterpillars, what is this sinister joke? Who are you? What did I do to you to bring me in such a place?"

"Oh, I'm an old friend of your parents, Miss Blackwell. If you are reasonable, we might reach a deal. However, if you are not – I'm afraid you will grace the obituary column of tomorrow's *London Journal*."

Think, Ivy Blackwell, think! They will never let you go alive knowing that you saw Lady Emmeline Asher! Just buy enough time and pray to all gods someone finds you!

"If you are after my parents' airship plans, I no longer have them. I have nothing to offer."

"I couldn't care less about your parents' airship. What I want is the method to produce the lifting gas which Chalford and Octavia discovered in their laboratory in Glenbuck. I tried to replicate it with my own means, but all my attempts were unsuccessful."

"I have no idea what you are talking about. My parents only gave me the airship plans, which we are using for a new prototype. They never talked about a lifting gas."

"Of course, it was a lucky coincidence that Jasper was chosen to design Her Majesty's new airship and picked you as his partner. It was then I understood I was tricked for almost three years, thinking that the Blackwells' work turned to cinders along with them. The papers have been with you all along."

"Whatever was in my parents' documents, I am certain they didn't want you to have them."

"They were stubborn and lacked a grand vision for the future – a pity, given their talents. Besides, they knew too much. I couldn't let them live knowing everything they did. I advise you not to follow their example."

Ivy stood motionless, fighting her urge to tear off her abductor's mask. The man was telling her that he killed her parents, and she could do nothing but stare at him, powerless and unable to save herself.

"For what you did to my parents and to those innocent people on *The Golden Griffin* who died that day, for what you are doing to me now – You will pay dearly!" Her voice was trembling despite her efforts. "When Jasper finds me, he will know what happened to his brother!"

"Jasper is probably too busy finding Lady Hollingsworth's criminal." He took out a pocket watch, looking at it quizzically. "She must be dead by now. Poor boy, I can't even start to imagine his pain. Do you really think he would spare a thought for you when his woman was killed?"

Ivy leaned against the wall, unable to speak. It was all too sudden, her entire world had been turned upside down too fast, and she couldn't understand what was going on. What did Rowena do wrong? Why did they have to murder her to keep Jasper's attention turned away?

The terrible truth dawned upon her. Mrs Carraway could never find her, and she had no one else to help her. She felt defeated. With or without the documents, that man would kill her.

She was alone.

~

"Master Asher, I'm afraid Madame is not 'ere, and I 'ave no idea when she's coming back." The Cinnamon Dove's doorman stared at him, unsure whether to invite him in or suggest he return at a more appropriate hour. The first option might bring Carmina's rage upon him, while the second might be too rude towards a nobleman.

"Madame told me to wait for her in her study." Jasper was in a hurry, so a little lie wouldn't harm anyone.

He rushed up the stairs without waiting for an answer. If Carmina was out, he could at least take the maps and go search for that underground entrance without her. He had to find Ivy and gather enough evidence for Edmund to act soon.

In Carmina's study, he went straight to the hidden drawer under her desk's countertop. He opened it easily – she kept the same cypher he had set when he first mounted it – but there was no map in there. He found her silver locket instead, which never left her neck, not even when she was out searching for information in her many disguises.

If she had let her precious locket there, something must have happened.

Its silver lid sprang open in Jasper's hand, revealing Edmund's rare smile.

15

"The problem with Carmina is that she considers herself invincible." Edmund stared at the silver locket Jasper had put on his desk, before slipping it into his pocket. His face was as expressionless as always, but the way he was pacing around his study in the Wyverstone mansion betrayed his distress. "I knew she would end up doing something like this. I did not want you to work with her precisely for this reason."

"I still fail to understand why she left on her own," Jasper said. "Everything went astray since last night. Rowena was stabbed, Ivy disappeared bloody hell knows where, Carmina decided to act alone, and I am going insane."

"Carmina did it for me," Edmund said, after a few moments of silence. He went to his favourite window wall encased in its intricate wrought iron frame. No lamp shone in the garden, and all he could see outside was thick darkness. "She left the locket so that no one could relate her to my name if she were caught. And went without you because she was afraid I could lose the only brother I have left. She promised me she would never put you in danger. This is how she is. And this is why I love her so much."

"Forgive me." Jasper still didn't dare look into his brother's eyes. "I was inconsiderate and cruel to say those things earlier. It never occurred to me that Carmina was your lover. Although it was quite obvious. You two always –"

"Enough of this." Edmund interrupted him, and Jasper didn't insist on the subject. "Our priority is to find Miss Blackwell tonight. Carmina surely went after her. If we find one, we find them both. I might dispatch my men sooner than I thought, but I need you to go there first and search for those two. Buy time until I arrive. Your priority is to keep them alive."

"But I don't have the bloody map any longer, so I don't see *how* I can find them! I don't have the slightest idea where the entrance is to the second underground level. When I searched with Carmina, we couldn't even find the entrance to the first one!" Jasper drank his brandy in one gulp, wiping his mouth with the sleeve of his white shirt. "Perhaps I should just pay Leythfordham a visit, beat the hell out of him and make him spit the contents of the map along with his teeth!"

"I have taken care of that matter without beating the hell out of him. Only that Leythfordham is not the owner of the hidden map you found in his house. He stole it."

Jasper stood motionless in the middle of the room. Suddenly, everything started to make sense.

"When I asked Hayes about the request for *The Skycradle* after Ivy's disappearance, Leythfordham's name came way too fast. Also, now that I think of it, he couldn't have commissioned the three workers who tried to rig Ivy's airship. Otherwise, he would have erased any trace that led him to them. His name was written in the Airharbour Assignments Office's ledger as if waiting to be discovered. Someone must have set him up. He is not the person we are looking for. Why would he steal that map, unless –"

"Unless he is not involved as we have thought, and he is only searching for his own answers. I started to have my doubts a while ago and realised he was the perfect puppet. Someone has been using him all this time, and I have reasons to believe my wife has the key to this riddle. You are finally coming to your senses, Jasper. Right when I was beginning to think I shouldn't have persuaded you to return into service."

"We are back to square one, and with no means to find Ivy and Carmina in the following hours." Jasper ran his fingers through his hair in frustration, searching his brain for an idea.

"Oh, not quite. You were too biased against Leythfordham, so I had another agent on him, who should be here soon. Wait for me downstairs. I shall call for Emmeline."

THE COTTON MASK COVERING Carmina's nose and mouth was far from enough to keep away the foul smell of the sewer water. She was treading warily through a maze of dump arched tunnels, making her way through the darkness with Jasper's torch. On some lengths, the sewage was high enough to flood the narrow rim, covering her skirts and boots up to her ankles.

It was one of the rare times she didn't need any disguise. That night, she only had two options – to succeed or die there. She had come as herself, with her tools of the trade hidden in the pockets of her long petticoats. The map she already knew by heart, which she kept inside her leather corset, rope, bullet pistol, paralysis pistol, and phials to charge it.

Whatever was coming her way, she was prepared.

Earlier that day, when Ginger had informed her about Ivy Blackwell's disappearance in Lady Emmeline Asher's carriage, she understood that the time for the showdown had come. She didn't trust the constabulary, and the Office of Classified Affairs never acted without substantial evidence, so she had to go alone. It was unfair towards Jasper, but when was life fair? At least he would be safe, and Edmund would be happy.

Carmina stopped in front of a round grilled gate, beyond which the tunnel was taking a descending course, and the sewer water got deeper. From a distance she could not guess, thumping noises echoed as if a horde of people were hammering into a large iron surface, making the mucky walls around her vibrate.

Closer. Push the gate and get closer.

She felt the bricks behind the grill until she found the latches that held it in place and pulled them open. The gate started moving with a rusty creaking sound, allowing her free passage to the other side of the tunnel.

Her skirts were wet up to the waist, and her clothes and lungs were impregnated with the foetid odour of the place. The darkness was diminishing, suppressed by a faint yellow light coming from far ahead.

If the map is accurate, I am close to Lady Hollingsworth's first school. Soon, I should be right under the Holborn skystation.

A sinister growl stopped her before reaching the end of the tunnel. A bark which reminded her of the dogs who had attacked Jasper in the courtyard of the derelict workhouse.

She took out her bullet pistol. At least she knew what to expect.

Or so she thought.

The massive black hound running towards her on

mechanical limbs was nothing she imagined. Sharp blades spurt out of its front knees. Blood and snoot were coming out through its fangs. It looked like the spawn of the darkest ring of hell.

"What in devil's name are you!"

The hound's speed was unlike anything she had seen before. She only had one moment to dodge it – and silently thank her reflexes and training in the process. With a steady hand, Carmina released the first bullet into the dog's shoulder.

The beast quivered, but steadied fast and jumped in her direction with an agonising howl, giving her just a split of a second to avoid it while falling on her back in the putrid sewer water. She threw away the soaked mask and spat, pulling the trigger again and discharging her pistol into the hound's head.

The beast fell over her in a lifeless lump, the blade on its knee cutting deep through her left arm. She bit her wrist to stifle a scream, her green eyes dilated with pain. With her good hand, she pushed her charge, who was lying with its mouth wide open and half of the face disfigured in a shapeless mash of blood and flesh.

Carmina tore the dirty sleeve, revealing her wounded arm. She tied the ripped cloth above the gash to stop the bleeding, then stood up, squinting. With her torch lost in the sewage, it was hard to distinguish the shadow that was coming towards her in the dim light.

"I was searching for the beast who escaped our laboratory and look what I find instead! A sewer rat! That mechanical hound was only an unfinished prototype, but it's still a wonder you could kill it. I gather you are not just an ordinary woman who got lost on her way to the laundry house, are you?"

The shadow became a man whose face was half covered by a leather mask, who was staring at her with a rifle in his hand. She knew what such a rifle could do. It was an enhanced version of her paralysis pistol, worse than death itself. Those who were hit by that thing lost their ability to move and remained crippled for life.

"No, not quite." Carmina grimaced in pain, but still couldn't help a sarcastic grin. "I would say an ordinary woman too curious to find out what brought down an entire building and a perfectly functional gondotram wagon."

"Well, lass, you either give us some reasonable justification of your presence or I shall have the pleasure to shoot you. I would gladly use this rifle on you right away, but it is not I who decides what to do with you. Now move."

He beckoned her to walk in front of him, nudging her with the rifle. They crossed the remainder of the tunnel until it forked into two separate ways. The man pushed her into the narrower one, which was going further down, where the light was coming from. At least it was dry, as the sewage kept flowing only through the main tunnel.

Filthy and dishevelled, soaked in the foul sewer water and with an arm dangerously close to infection, Carmina looked no better than a vagrant in the gutter when the man opened the iron door of an enclosure that resembled an observation room. A glass panel mounted into a wall revealed the hall below – a strange laboratory filled with all kinds of contraptions, glass recipients and tubes handled by a few masked people.

In a corner of the small enclosure, Ivy Blackwell was sitting on the floor, her hands tied in front of her. She was trembling, her face had lost colour, and her auburn hair had turned into a tangled mass of dirty locks. A middle-aged man whose face she couldn't see clearly was guarding her. He had the same long leather coat as the man in the tunnel, carried two pistols, and was camouflaged up to his eyes.

It would be hard to save the girl. But by no means impossible. She had thrown herself into the devil's den, and she would find a way out of there, come what may.

Carmina's captor went straight to the other man.

"Look what I found in the sewers," he said. "This rat killed the mech hound, so I brought her here. It was the only such beast we had, so Master will make some noise, I gather."

She bit her lip hard, trying to forget about the searing pain in her arm. Whatever happened from then on meant Ivy Blackwell's freedom and hers.

Or their death.

EMMELINE ENTERED THE SMALL PARLOUR, as impeccably dressed as ever, regardless of how late it was. Not even one strand of her hair was in disarray, not one fold of her skirts was astray. In the green dress that flattered her petite figure, with her blonde curls combed under a velvet headdress, she looked like an antique porcelain doll. She smiled at the two men, her eyes pinned on her brother-in-law.

"What a surprise!" Her thin voice was sending waves of anger through Jasper's brain. "I do hope nothing unpleasant happened for you to call on us at such an ungodly hour."

"My dear, let us skip these useless pleasantries, shall we?" Edmund's sharp tone startled even Jasper, who had not expected such a blunt approach. It was only then he understood his brother's dread. "You will take a seat and write in detail how we can reach the second underground level underneath the Holborn skystation. Followed by another thorough statement to explain why you ordered charcoal, saltpetre, and sulphur from the Glenbuck colliery three years ago – as I do not recall our household needing the aforementioned items. And why you kept ordering mine gas for three years. I am immensely interested in your pursuits in chemistry."

"Edmund, my love – Is anything the matter? I'm afraid I don't quite understand what you are asking of me."

"Perhaps these will freshen your memory. Oh, and do not use that word with me again. Love is the one thing this marriage never had."

As he was standing before his wife, tall and imposing, his blue eyes dark with a barely contained rage, Edmund seemed larger than life. He handed her the binder with all the documents Jasper had given him. Emmeline took the papers with trembling hands, her face turning ashen as she went through them. She looked around as if seeking the tiniest escape route, but she found none.

Through the glass wall of the parlour, the night seemed even murkier and heavier. The room itself had become an ominous entity, anticipating a looming disaster. Jasper was watching breathlessly, as if everything was hanging on Emmeline's answer.

"These are forged!" she shrieked, and Jasper couldn't tell what scared her more, the papers or her husband. "You cannot possibly believe such fabrications! How can a woman like me be involved in a trade with chemicals!"

"Dear sister, I am very curious about that as well. Your problem is that you never know when to stop. Try not to worsen things. They are already bad enough."

Jasper turned in the direction of the familiar voice, unable to hide his surprise. Oscar Bashford, the Duke of Herdforthbridge, was the last person he had expected to see that night in his brother's house.

"Right on time, Oscar," Edmund said. "I hope you brought that document. We need it tonight."

Edmund's words from earlier suddenly made sense in Jasper's mind. *I had another agent on him, who should be here soon.*

The duke was working for him.

Now, Herdforthbridge's impromptu piano concert in Leythfordham's house had an explanation. It was to help him.

I was too biased against Leythfordham, so you had Herdforthbridge tail the marquess. The duke could have been too biased towards his sister, so you had me tail Emmeline. You didn't trust either of us entirely. Brilliant, dear brother. Brilliant.

"I have his official testimony," the duke said. "Leythfordham is just a spineless coward, too eager to save his hide, so he spilt out everything he knew. Emmeline, do us all a favour and reveal whatever idiotic plan you are involved in. Your name is mentioned plenty of times in his statement, and I am eager to find out why. I understand you have been seeking the peers' support for his new airharbour, for which he had to sign and approve a lot of dubious papers for a lot of dubious activities. Such as providing support for Miss Blackwell's airship repair work. How do you explain that?"

"Oscar, I swear I would never –"

"Emmeline, I am in a hurry. Write what I asked." Edmund's voice was impatient and menacing, almost shaking with fury. It was the first time Jasper had seen such a raw reaction on his brother's face in public. "Deny or delay me any further, and I shall make sure you end up either in prison or at Bedlam."

"You wouldn't dare! Do not forget the power my family has! My brother is the Duke of –"

"Your brother is my close friend and a reasonable man!

Do not count on him to hide your crimes! Emmeline, who the hell are you covering for? Write those bloody instructions!"

"Do what he asked and stop using my name to threaten others!" The duke's voice was as commanding as Edmund's. "This is your only chance to find some leniency, as I do not intend to offer you any support."

"Care to tell me what is going on?" Jasper asked, still trying to process the newest of Edmund's well-hidden secrets.

"Oscar has always been my close friend," Edmund said. "I apologise for making you think otherwise, but it was necessary so that nobody suspected he was helping me with my work. The Marquess of Leythfordham is indeed involved, but only up to a point. I could not make a move without evidence, and now we have it. Thanks to you who brought those documents, and to Oscar who made Leythfordham talk. His testimony and Emmeline's are enough to send my men tonight."

Another memory came to Jasper's mind. After Edmund's marriage announcement, everyone stopped talking about how Herdforthbridge had waited in the church for a bride who never came. *The Golden Griffin* and conspiracies aside, the reason behind his brother's choice was simple. Edmund wanted to help his friend out of a terrible scandal, offering himself as the new epicentre of the *ton*'s gossip.

I misjudged you so much and for so long! How wrong I was to believe you are as cold and heartless as a stone!

"Here –" Emmeline spewed, handing the letter to her husband. "This is all I know. It is not much, as I was blindfolded before going underground. I went there only twice, and no further than the laboratory. But bear in mind, Edmund. I shall never forget this humiliation. Never!"

Edmund snatched the paper and read it hurriedly before passing it to the other two men.

"What in the devil's name is this!" Jasper was trying to make some sense of what he was reading. "Emmeline, what the hell is this madness? This – experiment? How many guards are down there?"

"There is no need for guards in that place," she said. "Not many people know what is happening there. They count on the fact that no one would ever find them in that cauldron of hell."

"Why are you involved in such enormity?" her brother asked. "An underground experimental laboratory without the approval of Her Majesty or even the Engineers Order? This is treason, for God's sake! Sedition!"

"Oscar, you have no care in the world other than your bloody books and music! Ignoring everyone, bored with everything, and playing your blasted piano, while the Orders will come to dictate everything. No wonder the woman who was to become your wife left you like a fool in the church! In our day and age, you do not strengthen a position such as yours with Nocturnes, but with action!"

Her hatred rolled out in full force, like the river water over a broken dam. Clenching her fists, with her beautiful face contorted with contempt, she had thrown away the mask of decorum and propriety that used to be everything to her.

"You are mad, Emmeline. But I don't have any time to waste on you," Jasper said. He turned to his brother, starting towards the door. "We still don't have any name or information about what these people are scheming, but at least now we know the way. Edmund, I'm going there first. I have no time to wait for you. If what Leythfordham and your wife wrote is true, those two are as good as dead in the sewers."

"I am coming as well," the Duke of Herdforthbridge said, to Jasper's surprise, who still couldn't get used to the idea that they were on the same side. "You need someone to watch your back."

Edmund stopped at the parlour door as they were leaving. The servants had long since gone to sleep, and the dark and empty vestibule had a foreboding aura in the dead of night.

"I am going to the Inspectorates to issue the written order, and I shall soon follow. Until we arrive, do everything in your power to keep those two alive."

"May I retire now?"

"No, Emmeline, you may not," Edmund said, without looking at his wife. "You are coming with me."

EDMUND DROVE his steammotor at full speed on the almost deserted streets of London, with the only goal of reaching his destination as hastily as he could. He needed all the composure he was capable of to hide the maelstrom of feelings tormenting him. What he'd always dreaded the most had materialised into a bleak reality.

In his mind, the possibility of Carmina being dead somewhere in a sewer underneath London was slowly turning into an unbearable certainty.

"What are you going to do with me?" Emmeline asked when the massive red brick buildings of the Inspectorates came into view in the distance. Her voice was feeble and unsteady, her fear almost becoming a physical presence in the narrow space between them.

"Unfortunately, nothing that I would like to," he said in a harsh, frightening tone. "You killed my brother and other seven people on *The Golden Griffin;* conspired against authority; and conducted illegal experiments. You also tried to frame the Marquess of Leythfordham and lied in a written testimony. I hope you don't expect me to believe you don't know who is behind that conspiracy. You deserve to be hanged. But it is not I who will decide your fate."

"I only agreed to sign the papers and facilitate the transactions, for no one would have ever suspected someone like me. Edmund, I swear I did not know they would blast *The Golden Griffin*! You must believe me!"

"Perhaps I'd have believed you if you stopped right after that bloody night!" Edmund shouted, unable to hold back any longer. "But you kept doing the dirty work of some bastards from the Engineers Order, giving them money and support right under my nose! I was a fool to underestimate you! To think you were a mere tool! What did they promise you? Emmeline, what was the price for your soul?"

"I *did* want to stop after *The Golden Griffin*," she said, and Edmund turned to her, surprised by her reaction. He had expected a fierce retaliation, yet he only saw a defeated woman with an unsteady voice and her eyes brimming with tears. "What happened terrified me so much! I wanted to tell you everything. I was scared, and I thought – I thought if I had you, it was enough. I could have done without all the power I was promised for my family and myself."

"Emmeline, do not play the victim. Your bloody lies and theatricals will not work on me. I happen to be in a terrible mood, so it would be wise of you to keep that little mouth of yours shut."

"You said love is the one thing this marriage never had." She kept talking, disregarding his warning. Something in her broken voice made Edmund look into her eyes, and that instant he knew she was honest. "You were wrong. I loved you enough to give up on everything I had set out to do. But that night – that cursed night after *The Golden Griffin*, you came to me drunk and called out another woman's name in my arms. It was then I realised you were using me, and I swore I would never forgive you. Oh, how I searched for that woman! For I wanted to know who was the one who thawed that awful heart of yours. But I never found her. I never found your *Carmina*."

She almost spat the name. Edmund stopped the steammotor on the paved lane in front of the Inspectorates, appalled. The memory of that night was still incomplete in his head. He remembered how he had drunk alone in his study after Jade's death; how he had gone to the Cinnamon Dove to see Carmina but never dared to enter; how he had returned home and sought solace in his wife's bed, the only warm thing in a house which had become too empty and cold. But he could never remember what happened there. Much less having revealed Carmina's name to her.

"That woman might be dead by now," he said curtly, avoiding an answer to her confession. "Come. You will spend a long night in this place, for you have many explanations to give. You will not leave until you write everything. A full statement about this plot, with all the names involved in it. I have my suspicions about the one who is pulling all the strings, but I want confirmation."

She didn't reply. Soon, they reached the Classified Affairs wing and Edmund's office.

He wrote the deployment order for his corps, then pressed the seal on his signature.

"You can sit there," he said, pointing to his desk. "I shall return soon, and I expect to find all the details I asked for. It is in your best interest to do as I say."

"Edmund, are you leaving me here? Alone in the Inspectorates? Where are you going?"

He locked the door without any other word.

The sound of his boots receded in the distance on the cold stones of the corridor.

16

"Again, who sent you here? This is the last time I'm asking nicely."

Carmina glared at the camouflaged man, a corner of her mouth lifted in a sarcastic grin. "Why is it so hard for you to accept that a woman can use her own brain?"

His fist landed against her jaw, filling her mouth with the metallic taste of blood. Her head resonated as if a host of bells were chiming inside her skull.

But she was no stranger to such punches. She had been trained for worse.

"Brazen harlot! Who told you about this place? Confess who sent you here, or I'll show you hell!"

"No one sent me here. Ask me a thousand times. My answer will not change."

This bastard knows nothing. What hell can be worse than my last three years?

Another punch, this time closer to her right eye, so forceful that she forgot about the wounded arm for an instant. Again, the taste of blood.

Left-handed, two bullet pistols. The other man only has the rifle. Do it now.

Closing her eyes, Carmina collapsed on the floor on her injured arm, swathed in a fresh wave of pain. If she wanted them to believe her, she had no choice but to grit her teeth and bear it.

"Rats and caterpillars! How could you hit her, you bloody animal!" Ivy shouted. "Damned barbarian! Abducting and beating women, without even the courage to reveal your face!"

"Oh, but you are so very wrong, Miss Blackwell," the man said. "I use this mask to protect myself from the foul chemicals in this place. If you behave, maybe I shall do you the courtesy of showing you my face."

His voice – He is not next to me any longer. If he is talking to Miss Blackwell, he is facing her.

Carmina opened her eyes, already forgotten by the two guards. One second was all she needed to take out her pistols and shoot one bullet in the camouflaged man's left hand, and a paralysis phial into the other one's leg, buying exactly fifteen minutes until the effect of the capsule vanished.

The man who had captured her stared with terrified eyes, unable to move, while the other one clutched his bleeding hand, crouching in pain. "Blasted slut, what have you done! Don't think you will get out of here alive!"

"Miss Blackwell," Carmina instructed, "take their weapons and bind them with this. I don't have enough strength at the moment."

She took out a small coil of rope from under her skirts and threw it to Ivy.

Shortly, both women were back into the labyrinth of sewers. They would be out in about one hour, provided that no one attacked them on the way.

But Carmina's work was far from finished.

"Who are you?" Ivy asked when they reached the first bifurcation. "How did you find me? I thought I wouldn't go out of that place alive."

"Carmina. A friend of Jasper's. Tell me, Miss Blackwell, do you know how to shoot?"

"I think I do."

She handed her the map, a torch she'd found in the observation room, and one of the pistols.

"Whatever comes your way, shoot without hesitation. Protect yourself. Follow this map, and you will be out soon. I still need to settle some things here."

Ivy took the weapon. "No. I'm coming with you."

My carriage stopped at Covent Garden, then I walked for a few minutes. I had a veil on my face so that no one could recognise me, and for the route to that place to remain a secret even for me. Afterwards, I tried to find it by myself, but I never could. We turned left in less than a minute and stopped after another few. I remember two entryways. One through the floor of a building and the other one through the pavement of the street. They uncovered my eyes only after they unlocked the cypher and opened an iron door, beyond which was pitch dark. One of my escorts pulled a rope. Then we waited until a wicker basket came up for us to descend.

JASPER HID EMMELINE'S note into his pocket. "Now it all adds up. The two entryways are actually one. She believed otherwise because her visits were before and after the building in her description fell."

"Lady Hollingsworth's school?" Herdforthbridge asked. "You think that is the entry point?"

"I am quite certain." Jasper was having a hard time accepting the duke as his partner. He particularly disliked hearing him utter Rowena's name, but it was neither the time nor the place for disagreement.

The ruins of Rowena's former school were dark and deserted. No one had bothered to clean the place, and, with so much rubble and so little time, finding the right spot was a challenge.

"I think I found it!" Herdforthbridge said from a corner close to the former privy, hardly containing his disgust. "Help me move the planks!"

They uncovered a hatch wide enough for a man to go through and descended, silently thankful that they didn't have to breathe the stench of mould and urine any longer.

In the overwhelming darkness, Jasper took out his torch, revealing a narrow corridor, so low that they had to crouch to cross it. He hesitated, unable to trust the duke. If that was a trap, he would die before having any chance to save Ivy and Carmina.

"Whatever is the matter?" The duke sounded as apprehensive as him. "We should reach the cyphered door soon. I suppose opening it won't be easy."

"They have yet to devise a cypher I cannot break," Jasper said, feeling the itch of the engineering challenge awaiting him.

There was no door handle. Instead, they found an iron wheel studded with numbered buttons and an intricate assortment of smaller cogwheels mounted at a short distance from one another. Jasper had never seen such a cypher and was tempted to reconsider his ability to unlock it.

"Hold this while I'm unlocking the bloody thing." He

handed Herdforthbridge his torch and squatted to work on the bizarre lock. "The correct sequence of numbers would push the cogwheels to engage and interlock so that the main wheel moves to release the door. I do not have time to figure out the algorithm, but I can force it open."

"This is why I don't like engineers. You complicate your existence too much. This ugly contraption is the embodiment of what I hate the most about your Order."

"Now you are starting to sound more like the Herdforthbridge I know," Jasper said while handling the cypher with the copper pin he always kept with him. "It's reassuring to see you are as insufferable as ever.

"I'm done," he added about a quarter of an hour later, stretching his back.

The door slowly slid to the left.

Jasper pulled the rope he found close to the door. He shut off his torch, waiting at the edge of the narrow shaft opening underneath. If Emmeline's words were true, a wicker basket would come up soon.

The muffled noises at the base of the shaft confirmed their expectations. The basket reached them before long.

"We don't know what is waiting for us down there." Jasper climbed into the basket. "I hope you can handle a pistol. Or a brawl."

They landed in front of two masked men who were too surprised to react at the sight of the intruders. Their hesitation was what Jasper and the duke needed to punch them so hard that they fell to the ground.

"I've had my share of fights," Herdforthbridge explained matter-of-factly, while gagging the watchmen with the sleeves of their own shirts. "Which way?"

"Can you hear those thuds? Whatever we are looking for, it must be there."

He lit his torch again and went into a narrow corridor which was going further down.

~

IVY FOLLOWED Carmina down the sewer, without knowing where they were going and with what purpose. She was tired, and longed to return to the outside world, to the safety of Lady Hollingsworth's mansion.

If only she could turn back time and stay home instead of brazenly breaking into Jasper's house! Had it not been for this strange woman, she might have been dead. As badly as she wanted to leave that place, she owed at least that much to her rescuer. Wounded and bleeding, with half of her face swollen, Carmina wouldn't make it by herself. Ivy was scared, but not a coward.

"Why are you going further in such a state?" Ivy asked, breaking the heavy silence. "You came here with a purpose, ain't it so? What are you looking for?"

"I'm afraid I cannot give you a straight answer. It might be something of great importance or nothing. We cannot know until we search every nook and cranny of this cave."

"Why are they after my parents' work? What is this place? Who are these people?"

"You are asking too many questions at once –" Carmina replied, her voice unsteady. "They want to replicate your parents' lifting gas but have no detail about it. What I am trying to find out is who *they* are and why they need that gas so badly. The answer must be here."

"Rats and caterpillars!" Ivy's anger was getting the better of her again. "How can something like this exist without the authorities' knowledge!"

"Well, Miss Blackwell, that is – Wait!"

She stopped where the tunnel turned right, prompting Ivy to do the same. Footsteps, and a faint trace of light. Whoever was coming, they would take them head-on.

Carmina sprang ready to shoot, only to run into Jasper and a tall blond man Ivy did not know.

"What in the devil's name are you doing here?" Carmina gritted her teeth, trying to keep her voice low.

Then she recognised the other man in the yellow glow of Jasper's torch.

"Herdforthbridge! You bloody bastard!" Ivy couldn't say whether Carmina was trembling with rage or with pain. "Jasper, why did you bring this traitor? Do you have any idea who he is?"

"He secured Leythfordham's testimony," Jasper said. "If Edmund trusts him, so should we."

"Carmina, you never let me explain, and I doubt a filthy sewer is a proper place for such a conversation," the blond man said. "Our activities here coincide, so it would be in everyone's best interest to work together."

"What the hell happened to you?" Jasper stared at her wounds, appalled. "Who did this?"

"I cannot say for sure, though I might have an idea." Carmina turned to Ivy without elaborating. "Miss Blackwell, please allow me to introduce Oscar Bashford, the Duke of Herdforthbridge. Take him with you and return to that laboratory. Make sure those two imbeciles are alive and well-guarded until we finish here."

Ivy nodded, glancing at the unknown man. If he came with Jasper, at least he was trustworthy. A part of her was still afraid, but she didn't have the luxury to choose.

~

"Miss Blackwell, you must have been through quite an ordeal. Perhaps it would be better if you returned first. I should manage very well on my own without putting you in more danger."

Ivy squinted at him, trying to figure out whether the duke was genuinely concerned or had ulterior motives to remain alone in the laboratory. Her instincts told her to trust him, but she was still cautious.

"Why is everyone in such a hurry to send me back all alone? I would be in more danger if I wandered around by myself. One thing I am certain of is that they would never let me return alive."

"As long as they need you, they won't kill you."

"Oh, but they would. I know my kidnapper's identity. I also saw this experiment lair – or whatever we should call it. Do you suppose they would let me go just like that?"

"No, they wouldn't. What do you mean you know your kidnapper's identity?"

"I do. We even had a little chat. The worst part is that she is Jasper's relative. I couldn't tell him earlier, but he will find out. His sister-in-law abducted me."

Herdforthbridge stopped, bewildered by that new piece of information he obviously did not expect.

"Are you certain it was Emmeline?"

"As certain as I am of my own name. Are you acquainted with that insufferable woman?"

"She is my sister."

It was Ivy's turn to be surprised, but she was starting to see the similarities. The elegant bearing, the handsome features, the aristocratic air.

Only that he was much more tolerable.

She recognised the iron door of the small observation chamber and pushed it open.

All they found was an empty room. They had come too late. The phial's effect had worn off.

"We didn't cross paths with those people, so they must have taken another route," the duke said. "Perhaps they went to inform their superiors about you and Carmina. Chasing them now would be useless."

Ivy agreed. "Let's find Jasper and Carmina. Wherever they are heading, they might use some help."

"Not before we see what this laboratory is about."

The duke strode to the rectangular window which revealed the hall below. Ivy joined him.

A vast and intricate network of huge brass pipes, pressure gauges, copper containers, wheels and faucets covered the entire area. Men wearing long white coats and leather masks swarmed among them, under the strict supervision of the guards.

"What the hell is this!" Ivy muttered. "Those must be scientists they brought for their experiments! I wonder what else is hidden here!"

"Herdforthbridge, what a surprise! You were the last person I expected to find here, given your well-known contempt towards the brilliant minds set to bend nature. I hope you are enjoying the view. For it is among the last ones you will ever see."

Ivy and the duke turned around, only to face the cold glitter of a paralysis rifle's muzzle pointed at them.

~

THE DISTANT THUDS had turned into deafening noises, as if thousands of enormous mauls were hammering into a metal wall with a thundering echo.

Jasper examined the map, trying to pinpoint their exact spot in the maze of tunnels.

"It unsettles me that we didn't meet anyone or anything along the way. If there was something else here apart from that laboratory, I gather it should have been guarded."

"Perhaps they never thought this place could be found," Carmina said. "Or that one of them could be a traitor. We need to be careful, though. They might keep other beasts around, ready to attack if they catch sight of us. Earlier I killed a hound – half animal, and half mechanical."

"Mechanical hound? What the bloody hell! They cannot make human automata, so they are experimenting on animals?"

"Jasper, you might have been right. There might be a connection between Humautomaton, the *Griffin*, and what is happening here. You should have seen that creature!"

"I am not looking forward to that." Jasper shivered. The memory of a similar hound attacking him was still vivid in his mind. "Here, this should be the entrance we are searching for."

The tunnel was dry, the sewage following its flow elsewhere. Its foul smell had vanished, replaced by the odour of humid stone and mould. They stopped next to the round vent of a duct that spiralled deeper into the underground, letting out a strong stench of chemicals and tar.

Jasper crouched and looked, but the torch only revealed pitch-black darkness.

"I cannot see the other end, but it seems an exhaust tube." He turned to Carmina, trying to assess her state. "This is our only way further. Do you think you can make it?"

She nodded, and Jasper slid through, controlling his movement downwards with great difficulty. If it was that hard for him, he could only imagine how it was for Carmina. The bleeding had stopped, but the wound was raw and ugly, and she could barely move her arm. But it was too late to give up, and she wouldn't even if she could.

Their descent didn't last for more than a minute. The duct ended onto a narrow metallic landing with no railing, which surrounded a vast circular cauldron like a belt. The air was so toxic that it became almost unbreathable. Huge bulbs mounted into the cavernous walls flooded the space with electric light.

Jasper and Carmina jumped off the duct on the landing and crawled towards the edge to look below, careful not to be seen.

"What in the devil's name are they making here?" Carmina asked through gritted teeth. "It looks like an airship. But a rather strange one."

"That's because it is a war airship. I have never seen anything like this! I'm afraid to even think of its purpose!"

Jasper stared at the scene with a mixture of terror and awe. A colossal airship painted in black, with an enormous golden kraken embossed on her, filled most of the cavern. A myriad of grapples coming down from the domed stone ceiling supported her envelope, which was so big it could hold a regiment. Its lower half was fitted all around with retractable windows for the crew quarters.

A row of cannons surrounded the massive gondola.

She looked less like an airship and more like an odd war machine.

All the answers Jasper had been searching for finally had a shape. He clutched the landing's edge, unable to take his eyes off the peculiar craft. "Now I know why they were so desperate to secure the formula for the Blackwells' lifting gas! Why those incidents in St. Giles happened! It was because of *this thing*! They must have tested it at least twice. Once when Rowena's building collapsed, and the second time when the gondotram wagon fell. The shockwaves of the tests reverberated above!"

Below, people were scurrying all over the place or working on the unfinished craft, their faces hidden behind leather masks. Next to the generator, Jasper noticed an installation of boilers and pressure gauges mounted on a platform. Thick ducts connected them to the airship's envelope.

"The laboratory is the experiment room," Carmina said. "They are trying to replicate the gas for this airship. If they are so desperate as to abduct Miss Blackwell, they must be planning to use this monster soon. How are we going to stop them?"

"I hope you don't mean *us* stopping them, for this is something you and I alone cannot do. Edmund will be here before long, so it would be wiser to wait for him. Until then, let's go back to that bloody sewer."

Carmina nodded, and they started towards the duct.

"Well, well, a lot of unexpected guests tonight. You even brought down two of my men. I'm afraid I cannot let you return, but I'll give you a couple of friends of yours to keep you company until I send you all to the netherworld."

Jasper stood up and turned, his eyes wide in shock at the familiar voice. On the same landing, Benedict Quimby, Senior Lord of the Engineers Order, was pointing a pistol to Ivy Blackwell's temple, pushing her close to the landing's edge. Both Ivy and the Duke of Herdforthbridge had their mouths gagged and their hands tied at the back.

He saw how frightened Ivy was, and suddenly remembered Rowena's ghastly face, her doctor's words, the people who were dying in agony in the street after the gondotram fell, their cries while begging the nurses to save their lives.

An impending wave of rage was turning into a palpable presence in his chest. He wanted to beat the man senseless, but he didn't have the upper hand.

If Edmund didn't come soon, all four of them would die.

"Benedict Quimby, don't you dare lay a hand on them! What you are doing is treason, and you will rot in gaol! The Inspectorates are on your tail."

For one instant, he thought he saw a glint in his eyes, but it was too fast to be sure.

"This place can accommodate plenty of guests," he said. "But they should be aware of one thing. Whoever comes here, never returns. Regardless of who they are."

"Bloody bastard, you betrayed the Order! I respected you, but you are rubbish!" Jasper shouted. "You will kill everyone who is working here, aren't you? Who are these people?"

"They were lucky I chose them. Else, they would beg for work at the docks or the airharbour! I sent money to their families, who would squirm in misery if not for me. Their meagre lives are mine. I *own* them! It is an insignificant price to pay for the great deeds I'll accomplish for this country."

"*This* is the factory where everyone kept disappearing!" Jasper said. "You brought them here to make this airship! You never intended to let them return to their families!"

Carmina clasped her wounded arm, her face as pale as a ghost. "Quimby, you are insane! But I shall not let the likes of you kill other innocent people!"

One moment later, a capsule left her paralysis pistol.

The phial sank into Ivy's shoulder.

"Did you think I would fall for that little stunt?" Benedict Quimby bellowed, pushing Ivy's inert body over the landing. "Now give me all your weapons, else I'll –"

The unexpected pain in his legs made him falter. In his rush to turn Ivy into his shield, he hadn't noticed the look Carmina exchanged with Herdforthbridge. The duke moved behind him, kicking him in the back of his knees.

Carmina sent another phial in Quimby's direction, too swiftly for him to react. This time, he collapsed with a scream, his body limp and powerless.

Jasper froze in horror, too afraid to look down. A thousand images of Ivy dead and mutilated filled his mind, overlapping with the image of his twin brother burnt and maimed.

He wanted to run without looking back.

A slap on his shoulder brought him to reality.

"Come to your senses, for God's sake!" the duke barked, his mouth and hands freed. "This is not the time to turn into a frightened porridge!"

Carmina bent over the landing. Everyone had stopped their work, surrounding the boilers where Ivy had fallen, unsure of what to do.

"She is alive!" Carmina said. "The distance is not deadly! She fell on the main duct and from there onto the platform! I'm going to her!"

Jasper looked over the landing, while Carmina went down. Ivy was unable to move, her eyes wide with dread. Her leg was injured, but she was in one piece. In a quarter of an hour, the phial effect would vanish, and she would be back.

"Central gauge failure!" a voice from below warned. "The pointer is blocked, and the boiler pressure is increasing! The duct's pressure valve stopped working after this woman fell on it!"

"Turn off the boiler!" Jasper said. "Don't let the pressure rise!"

"I hope you don't expect a bloke like him to know how to

work with that installation!" Benedict Quimby was laughing hysterically, looking like a grotesque fat worm who could only move his head. "No one but me manages it! Let's see how good of an engineer you are, Jasper! If you deserve to be the next one in command!"

Jasper jumped off the landing and went straight to the boilers.

The cause was most likely either the vibrations or the steam, not Ivy. I need to switch off the entire system.

He only had a few minutes to figure out how.

"You lot! Unlatch the ducts off the envelope to release the pressure! Disengage quickly!"

The few men next to the ducts were gawking at him, unable to understand what was going on.

"Listen to him!" One of them took one step closer, and Jasper recognised Hector's voice behind the leather mask. "He is Master Jasper! I know him from the Copper Kettle! He can get us out of here! Do as he says!"

"Wait!" Ivy shouted from the spot where she was trapped. "Are you going to release all that steam in here? Are you mad? What if you cannot turn off the boiler? We will all die!"

"If I cannot turn it off, we shall die anyway, with or without disengaging the ducts. Only the manner will differ. Ivy, I need you to trust me! I shall find a way!"

Everyone disappeared to do as they were told, while Jasper found the two central knobs enclosed in a small glass case hidden under the main pressure gauge. One of them stopped the boilers, and the other instantly increased the pressure to blow up the entire thing. The Engineers Order used to place such identical knobs in many of their inventions, to protect their patents.

Finding the correct one was a matter of pure luck.

I cannot do this – I must not do this! I should not gamble with these people's lives!

"Quimby! Which one is it?"

"The one on the left! Hurry, or this place will blow up like *The Golden Griffin*!"

Jasper, think! Such a coward would not kill himself! He only waits for the paralysis phial's effect to wear off.

Yet something in his voice didn't convince him.

Whoever is building such an airship almost one hundred feet underneath London is not in his right mind. He would blast himself along with the entire thing rather than being caught.

A hand squeezed his shoulder, and he turned to see Carmina.

"Trust your instincts, Jasper. You are an excellent agent and engineer. It is time you remembered that."

Her trust offered him the reassurance he so much needed. He closed his eyes and pulled the knob on the right side of the glass case.

For one second, time stopped.

The only sound that Jasper could hear was the beating of his own heart, stifling all the other noises, making him feel like he was floating between life and death.

Until he heard his brother's voice.

"Benedict Quimby, Senior Lord of the Engineers Order, you are arrested for high treason and conspiracy against Her Majesty, the Queen of England; for abducting innocent citizens; for murder; and for endangering public order."

Jasper jumped on a duct to have a clearer view of what was happening. Both the landing above, and the space around the airship were full of Edmund's men, dressed in their green and brown uniforms, wearing leather masks, and pointing their rifles.

"The rats from the Classified Affairs!" Quimby spit. "How

in the devil's name did you come here? The entrance could only fit one man!"

"We used the one through the old workhouse. Now I understand why you insisted on keeping that building as it was. You lied that you would use it for the Order, but you needed it to hide your lair."

"Not many people knew of that place, yet you managed to find it. You are good, Wyverstone. I knew why I was afraid of you. I was counting on Emmeline to keep an eye on you, but I was wrong to trust her. If she cannot even seduce her husband, she is worthless."

What none of them expected was Herdforthbridge's fist landing hard against his jaw.

"Don't you dare speak about my sister in that manner, you filth! You are to blame for whatever she did! Had it not been for you, she would have never been part of this!"

"She was part of this because she saw the future better than any of you! The future belongs to the Orders, without any interference from the Royal House! The Queen pretends to support progress, but she still wants to control everything. With her authority gone, we can evolve even further! We do not need anyone to limit our experiments based on the old-fashioned ethics of morality. Science does not need that!"

"Humautomaton. It wasn't Leythfordham's experiment, but yours. All along. You could never get over your grudge for that rejection and wanted to push Her Majesty out of your way. But tell me one thing." Edmund's voice was looming and dangerous. "Why did you blast *The Golden Griffin*?"

"The Blackwells knew about Humautomaton and what I wanted to do. That I wanted to make the most amazing war airship to take over England and beyond! I thought that innovative minds such as theirs would understand, but they didn't. Of course, I couldn't let them live. They knew I wanted to change the state of things in England, to give absolute power to the Engineers Order. I did not intend to kill Jade, but I had no choice. Herdforthbridge almost thwarted my plan when he told Leythfordham something was happening. Remember, Your Grace?" He turned his head to the duke with a sarcastic look. "*That ship must not fly*. This is what you told him. I am not sure what you sniffed about that, but the Marquess alerted me, thinking he was saving the day. Fools like him come in handy."

"So, you used him!" Jasper returned onto the landing, leaving Carmina with Ivy. Edmund had asked the question he had been too afraid to utter, clinging to his last straw of sanity. If he had confronted Quimby about *The Golden Griffin* himself, he would have killed him. "You promised him support for his airharbour because *you* needed to tear down an area large enough for your war airship to go up.

"Only that your big ugly monster would not go up without the new lifting gas. You almost killed Ivy, fearing she might know the truth. You killed innocent people in that gondotram fall! You scheduled the tests for the cannons when the gondotram was in Holborn! You rigged the wagon so that it wouldn't remain stuck on the tracks but fall due to the shockwaves. Thus, you offered Leythfordham a reason to ask for evacuation! Because *you*, and not him, needed to clear the former rookery! You killed my brother! Bloody murderer!"

His eyes were bloodshot, and his voice had become a frantic howl. He darted towards Quimby with a blood-curdling scream. The duke caught him, holding his arms in a clasp of steel.

"Jasper, you have no right to exact justice," Edmund said. "Leave that to the authorities. Take Benedict Quimby!" he ordered, turning to his men. "Make sure you leave no one here. Seal this place and keep it guarded! We shall return to investigate."

"Too late, Wyverstone!" Benedict Quimby shouted while the guards were seizing him. "You may arrest me today, but you cannot change the future! It belongs to the Orders, to science! They will one day replace the established status quo, and that day will come sooner than you think!"

"We ought to go down," Jasper said, still shaking. "Ivy and Carmina are there. They went through a lot. It's a wonder they are still on their feet."

"You aren't going anywhere until you come to your senses. Wait for us here."

From where he was crouched, close to the edge, Jasper saw Edmund jumping off the landing, followed by the Duke of Herdforthbridge. They ran to Ivy and Carmina, who were limping towards them leaning on one another.

Jasper watched how his brother carried Carmina in his arms, while the duke was supporting Ivy. The paralysis phial's effect had gone, but her muscles were still weak.

It's over. Jade, now that your murderer is in our hands, do you think I could move on? Would you allow me to move on? Would you allow me to leave the nightmare of the past three years behind?

EPILOGUE

London, August 1895

Jasper opened the windows, breathing in the crisp air of that particularly pleasant morning. A mild sun was bathing his chamber in a bright glow, as cheerful as the voices coming from the docks.

He dressed and went downstairs. He ate quickly, then took the leather tubular case containing *The Cerulean Lady*'s plans and drawings.

Soon, he was on his way to Rowena's school opening ceremony, the first stop on that important day. After almost three weeks, she could resume her social pursuits. Jasper knew she had chosen that date on purpose. It was the same day he and Ivy presented their airship at the Engineers Order assembly.

The three of them would share a treasured memory.

A crowd had gathered in front of the school, near the tables. Jack Killen and his children, Hector, and all his other friends from the Copper Kettle. Everyone was thrilled. Not only for the food and drinks, but also to celebrate Lady Hollingsworth's return.

He was surprised to see Carmina there, engaged in conversation with Ivy. She had recovered well, her face had no trace of bruises, and the sleeve of her blue dress hid the scar on her arm. She didn't even glance at Edmund, who was talking to the Duke of Herdforthbridge nearby. They kept quiet after the events in the underground, where she had almost died.

However, her silver locket, which Jasper had last seen disappearing into Edmund's pocket, had returned around her neck.

Neither she nor Edmund were the most talkative persons when it came to their private lives. Edmund was going through a difficult divorce, for which he took the blame entirely upon himself. Whether he did that out of pity for Emmeline or out of friendship for the Duke of Herdforthbridge, Jasper couldn't say.

"Lovely day, isn't it? I am so happy you came!"

Jasper turned towards Rowena's smiling face, which he once feared he would never see again.

"I would have come even if it meant delaying my presentation."

He took a small pendant out of his pocket.

"What is this?" Rowena asked, while he folded her fingers around the trinket. "It looks like your contraption in Seven Dials."

"Only much smaller," he said. "I made it as a present for you, for this day, and for what you are doing for these people. So that you can always see the time and the cardinal directions. If you are ever lost, to always find your way back."

Her bright smile was the only gratitude he needed. He couldn't make his feelings clear to her, but he was certain she understood. Be it twenty years or a day, he would be by her side for whatever time she had left.

"Lady Hollingsworth, allow me to congratulate you." Herdforthbridge came to greet her, along with Edmund. "You turned a wrecked warehouse into a functional establishment, which is nothing short of amazing. I was going to take it down and use the land for other purposes."

"What greater purpose can it have than helping the less fortunate? No words would be enough to thank you for donating this building, Your Grace. It was an immense help I had never dared dream of."

Jasper finally understood why the duke – who never mingled with the lower class – was there.

"Edmund came up with the idea, but the result exceeded our expectations," the duke said. "This establishment looks quite decent."

"That's because all the people here made it so." Everyone's eyes turned to Ivy, who had just joined their circle. She was wearing a new aeronaut gear and had tied her red curls in a thick ponytail, with her goggles clasped tightly on her head as usual. She had returned to her house but was still visiting Rowena regularly. As different as they were, they had become friends.

"Miss Blackwell, when are you going to stop dressing like a pirate and try a ladies outfit for a change? You look like you are going to raid an airship," Herdforthbridge said, but he was amused rather than reprimanding.

For one second, Jasper was tempted to think Ivy was another reason for his presence, but he quickly dismissed the absurd thought.

"Never, Your Grace," Ivy retorted, glaring at him. "I would suggest you keep your fashion related guidance for yourself. Or for whoever needs it. Which is not I."

"Are you ready?" Jasper asked, before Ivy's temper could be challenged any further. "We should go now if we don't want to be late."

Ivy grinned and took his arm. Shortly, they were on their way to the Inspectorates in Westminster.

~

THE FIRST FLOOR, assigned to the Orders, was in uproar when Jasper and Ivy arrived. The assembly was an important event in itself, organised only twice a year, but that one's special circumstances put it on a different scale of significance.

Benedict Quimby's imprisonment had turned the entire Order upside down, so Master Hollingsworth was acting as temporary Senior Lord until the Engineers World Gathering in spring. Given the current state of affairs, he was the only person who had both the experience, and the Queen's trust for the position. Edmund had started investigating all the members, to discover how far Quimby's plot had reached. Until the inquiry was over, no one could be elected as full Senior Lord.

Jasper was determined to have their project approved. If all went well, the following spring they would see *The Cerulean Lady* soaring high in the skies of London before the eyes of the world's most prominent engineers. Which would be the most appropriate way to honour Octavia and Chalford Blackwell's memory and make his and Ivy's work known.

When everyone was seated in the amphitheatre, he went to the dais alongside Ivy. They stopped in front of the cork board where he had pinned the sheets of paper containing their drawings and plans.

"Honourable gentlemen," he said, taking Ivy's hand, "before proceeding with the engineering design you are all expecting, please allow me to introduce my colleague. She contributed greatly to the successful completion of the project I shall bring to your attention. This is Ivy Blackwell, daughter of late Octavia and Chalford Blackwell, whose discovery we used in our enterprise."

The murmur created by the unexpected guest soon receded, and Jasper began talking, taking turns with Ivy. While the words were rolling out of his mouth, he relived all the events of the past months. The day he first met Ivy; the night he had flown *The Skycradle;* their trip to Scotland; the experiments in the Blackwells' laboratory in Glenbuck; his return into the service as an agent and the investigations with Carmina; Rowena on the brink of death; the terrible night they discovered Benedict Quimby's installation underneath London.

He felt alive. He had returned where he belonged. For the first time in three years, his heart was light, released from the heavy burden he had carried since Jade's death.

"Therefore, *The Cerulean Lady* will be not only the first airship of such size, the first airship with a double-tiered open space gondola, and a heating system never attempted for a craft. She will also be the first one to use laevium as lifting gas, which makes possible all the aforementioned features. Given its innovations, I daresay this engineering project will bring England into the attention of the entire world again."

When he finished, the audience was silent. Were they convincing enough? Had everyone understood the potential of such a prototype? Will *The Cerulean Lady* have a future?

The sudden burst of applause that followed gave him the answer and the reassurance he needed. Their airship would see the light of day.

"Honourable gentlemen, if you all agree, we should start

voting," Theophilus Hollingsworth said. "Unless there are further questions, of course."

"I do have a question." The Marquess of Leythfordham stood up, glaring at Jasper. "This is indeed a great proposal. However, I believe it is unrealistic. If we want to make this new lifting gas usable, we must produce it on a large scale. The construction of the works would take a considerable amount of time. It cannot be completed on time for the Gathering."

"What if we use a building that already exists?" Jasper countered. "I am thinking of the former workhouse in St. Giles. It is big enough to accommodate a factory and would also provide work for many residents in the area. Benedict Quimby secured it for the Order, so it will be the Order's decision whether we can use it for such purpose."

"Both issues will be subject to the members' vote!" Theophilus Hollingsworth beckoned the Marquess of Leythfordham to take his seat, and the voting began.

Almost everyone was in favour of both *The Cerulean Lady* and the proposal for the laevium works.

"I humbly thank you for your trust," Jasper said. "However, I have a request before proceeding further with this project.

"Miss Blackwell is an excellent aviator." He kept talking, under everyone's scrutiny, including Ivy's. "Yet, she is not part of any Order. Not because she lacks the skills, but because she lacks the financial means and the appropriate support. I am asking you to extend a recommendation letter to the Aviators Order to include her in their ranks. It is the least we can do to repay her parents' invaluable contribution. I invoke the Mutual Confidence Article among the Orders."

"Jasper, I'm afraid this will be difficult," his master said. "You must not forget that the Order issuing the request is the warrant of those they recommend. If something happens, the Engineers Order will be held accountable. The Mutual Confidence Article must be invoked only when your trust in that person is absolute."

"Miss Blackwell gave us her parents' most important work. The papers everyone else considered lost on *The Golden Griffin*," Jasper said. "She could have sold them *to any country* for an insane amount of money. Yet she agreed to use them for Her Majesty's airship. That alone should be convincing enough. I guarantee for her with my membership and all the patents I own."

"YOU ARE NOW an official member of the Aviators Order," Jasper said, poking Ivy's shoulder. "Worry not, they will accept. The Article is rarely invoked, and it can never be turned down."

"Thank you, Jasper." She was staring at the perpetual flow of water tumbling down the giant copper wheel of the waterfall in the Inspectorates' garden. "I shall not disappoint you."

"Of course. We need to organise a factory and build an airship. That is no small matter."

He looked at the sky above, punctured by three small airships flying close to the Westminster Tower.

In about a year, The Cerulean Lady will take to the skies. I shall guide her until that day comes, until I see her airborne. It will be a long way, but I am patient. I have just returned.

AUTHOR'S NOTE

Thank you for reading *Laevium*. For a lot of reasons, this is a story very dear to me, and my first pursuit as an author in the steampunk world, a fandom which I have been following for many years. I hope you enjoyed it, and, if you are curious about the future endeavours of Jasper and his friends, they will be revealed in the following two novels of *The Cerulean Airship* series, *Engineerium* and *Caelium*, with more challenges and foes to face.

It would be lovely if you could spare a moment to leave a review on your favourite retailer's website. I would also love to keep in touch. You can find me at www.delifictional.com and on Twitter (@RuxandraTarca), where we can talk about books and all things steampunk and Victorian.

ACKNOWLEDGMENTS

Writing *Laevium* was an amazing, yet challenging journey, which I could have never accomplished if not for the wonderful people who supported me along the way. I am grateful for everything they have given me, and I want to thank them properly. A heartfelt thank you to my sister Monica Tarca, who believed in me and in this novel, and always encouraged me; to Alina Popovici, one of my best friends, who created a stunning cover for this book, but also kicked me harshly when necessary, and was the ruthless critic I needed to make this story the best I could; to Rose Green, whose precious suggestions and corrections helped me greatly; and to all my lovely friends and valuable beta readers. I cannot thank them enough for their feedback and encouragement.

Made in the USA
Las Vegas, NV
03 October 2021